Jacuzzi

Written by
Hannah Bos & Paul Thureen

Developed by
Oliver Butler

Made by
The Debate Society

A SAMUEL FRENCH ACTING EDITION

SAMUEL FRENCH

FOUNDED 1830

SAMUELFRENCH.COM
SAMUELFRENCH-LONDON.CO.UK

ISBN 978-0-573-70430-7

www.SamuelFrench.com
www.SamuelFrench-London.co.uk

FOR PRODUCTION ENQUIRIES

UNITED STATES AND CANADA
Info@SamuelFrench.com
1-866-598-8449

UNITED KINGDOM AND EUROPE
Plays@SamuelFrench-London.co.uk
020-7255-4302

Each title is subject to availability from Samuel French, depending upon country of performance. Please be aware that *JACUZZI* may not be licensed by Samuel French in your territory. Professional and amateur producers should contact the nearest Samuel French office or licensing partner to verify availability.

MUSIC USE NOTE

IMPORTANT BILLING AND CREDIT REQUIREMENTS

JACUZZI was commissioned by Ars Nova (Jason Eagan, Artistic Director) in New York, NY and premiered there in October, 2014 with scenic design by Laura Jellinek, costume design by Jessica Ford, lighting design by Bradley King, sound design by M.L. Dogg, prop design by Noah Mease and production stage management by Lisa McGinn. The Production Manager was Jes Levine, the Assistant Stage Manager was Laura Kim, the PA was Jenny Gorelick, and the Assistant Directors were Hunter Bird and Kate Hopkins. It was directed by Oliver Butler. The cast was as follows:

HELENE . . . . Hannah Bos

ERIK. . . . . Paul Thureen

BO. . . . . Chris Lowell

ROBERT. . . . . Peter Friedman

JACUZZI was developed as part of the Ars Nova Artist Retreat at Vineyard Arts Project, Edgartown, MA: Ashley Melone, Founder and Artistic Director.

JACUZZI was also developed in association with the Almeida Festival 2013 and with support from The Ground Floor at Berkeley Repertory Theatre, Berkeley, CA.

JACUZZI was supported by a Jerome Foundation 50th Anniversary Grant.

Commissioned and Developed by Ars Nova
Jason Eagan, Artistic Director; Jeremy Blocker, Managing Director
World Premiere produced by Ars Nova
511 West 54th Street New York
www.arsnovanyc.com

CHARACTERS

WOMAN/HELENE – seems to be early to mid 30s – Long-haired, slightly hippie-ish-looking drifter who enjoys being in other people's homes. And being other people.

MAN/DEREK/ERIK – seems to be mid to late 30s – "Helene's" friend and partner. A presence so calm and quiet…you don't realize he's standing right behind you.

BO ELDER (ROBERT JR.) – 26 – Attractive, sensitive, damaged son of Robert Elder.

ROBERT ELDER (SR.) – Psychologist who made a fortune writing parenting books (along with his now ex-wife) based on experiments he did on his son Bo. Always talking.

PRODUCTION NOTE
FROM THE DEBATE SOCIETY

Hi! We're the Debate Society. Hannah and Paul are writers and act in the plays, and Oliver is the director and develops the plays with them. We are very excited that you are reading *Jacuzzi* and will be even more excited if you decide to produce it. This note is intended to make your show as awesome as possible. Due to spoilers, you might want to read this note after you read the play. Up to you.

First off: the Jacuzzi. Don't be afraid of using a real hot tub. We found one that looked like new that was actually from the early 1990s. There are a lot of people trying to get rid of hot tubs, and because they are hard to dispose of, you can probably get a good deal or get one for free locally if you handle the delivery. Also, most hot tubs are self-contained. Make sure your floor can sustain the weight, then put it in place, fill it up, plug it in, and there you go! With all the getting in and out water does spill, so it's helpful to lay down some waterproof material under the floorboards when installing the set. You are going to want to spend some time getting the chemicals right. We ended up doing a total water change every week to keep it crystal clear. Also, don't let the designers and director jump in in their t-shirts and underwear after a long tech. Clothes have trace amounts of detergent in them and it will lead to a neverending bubble bath.

While you shouldn't be afraid of using a real jacuzzi, we did workshops of the play in London and at Berkeley Rep with a fake jacuzzi – or "Faux-cuzzi," which was basically a plywood box with benches inside. Then we relied on sound design to create the "bubbles" and lights for "water." It was fun to imagine those elements, and ultimately not what we wanted to do…but might be fun to try in a stripped-down production. In general though, if it's doable, water on stage is really great.

When we made this play we were very interested in a passive kind of lying where you essentially let other people lie for you...largely by saying nothing so that others fill in the gaps in your story. With Helene and Erik, we created characters who generally go with the story that they are handed, or take pieces of other people's stories and repurpose them into their own lives. A lot of the fun of this play is watching how Helene and Erik's roles change as Bo and Robert make assumptions about them and who they are. These shifts should be simple and subtle. They are good at what they do, and calmly enjoy the game of it all. When Robert mistakenly calls Derek "Erik," they just go with it. Then we watch Bo's confusion after he tries to correct his dad. All these little lies don't all add up to one perfect lie – they should accumulate so that by the time the play is in full swing, we know that the whole world is a complex web of fictions. In a few spots, where we've felt it was particularly important, we added stage directions indicating things like quick glances between Helene and Erik. This isn't comprehensive; it's up to you to find all the ways the characters watch and react to each other. The more private little connections and negotiations, the better. The play is a world of subtle shifts in power and gamesmanship...make those shifts smooth and the characters authentic and real and the audience will lean in and enjoy tracking what's going on as Helene and Erik begin to puppet an unexpected father/son reconciliation. There is sweetness there...but always an underlying slow-burn menace.

Erik's hair and Helene's tooth. In our production Erik had long stringy hair and Helene had one discolored tooth. These elements don't work if they're done too broadly. A bad wig and a black tooth and the whole thing looks like a clown show. The key is to make Helene and Erik look simultaneously reliable and dangerous. In one light they look sort of folksy and in another, like predators. Erik's wig needs to be really great. Our wig designer, Dave Bova, created a piece that looked so real there was always a gasp from the audience when Paul pulled it off, as no one knew it was a wig. Hannah started experimenting with one off-color tooth – which we lovingly called "Funky Tooth." It really gave her smile a sort of disarming, off-kilter quality – but also felt like there might be something dead in there.

The End. In the last scene, when the tub is covered for the first time, it presents a mystery and you want the audience to begin to wonder, "Wait...what's in the Jacuzzi?" Is Bo dead in the Jacuzzi? Yes, we think so. And most audience members thought so as well. But it's perfectly OK for audience members to have other interpretations...it makes for great post-show conversation!

THE DEBATE SOCIETY WOULD LIKE TO THANK:

Jason Eagan, Emily Shooltz, Renee Blinkwolt, Casey York, Lee Ann Gullie, Claire Graves, Burton Frey, Eric Shethar, Reed Whitney and entire staff or Ars Nova, The Affordables, Hannah Andrews, Annie Baker, Kyle Bancroft, Marge Betley, Jeremy Blocker, Charlene Bos, Dave Bova, Maggie Buchwald, Isaac Butler, Nora Sorena Casey, Hanna Cheek, Alison Clarke & Jay Yates, Margot Connolly, Eric Cotti, Michael Cyril Creighton, Cynthia Crossen & James Gleick, Mateo Ervin, Jonathan Ehrlich, Jody Falco & Jeffrey Steinman, Jocey Florence, Cynthia Flowers, Andrew Garman, Jenny Gersten, Di Glazer, Kristin Goehring, Sam Gonzalez, Adam Greenfield, Gabrielle Hamilton, Hartig-Hilepo, Jessica Hecht, Josh Henderson-Cox, Frank Holzubiec, Andy Horwitz, Grace Interlichia, ICM, Jillian Jetton, Lisa Kron, Sarah Lazarus, Natalia Lopresti, Lyndsay Magid, Anne Love, Steve & Carolyn McCandless, Olivia McGiff, Susan Medak, Brian Mendes, Ashley & Brittany Melone, Chris Morriss, Mina Morita, Lucy Morrison, Keith Nobbs, Casimir Nozkowski, The O'Connell Family, Madeleine Oldham, Becky Parker Geist, Willie Reale, Mark Rossier, Ian Savage, Eleanor Savage & the Jerome Foundation, Felice Shapiro & Bill Cress, Hanlon Smith-Dorsey, Leslie Strongwater, Mark Subias, Michael Suenkel, Tony Taccone, Dawn Taylor, Jeanine Tesori, Evan Thayer, UTA, Tory Vazquez, Rachel Viola, Melissa Wells, Danny Wolohan, Doug Wright & David Clement, Pia & Jimmy Zankel.

To Jason and Emily

(1991. The living room of a private ski in/ski out chalet located on the mountainside above a small Colorado resort town. Inside the room: a brand new Jacuzzi, early '80s TV, a stereo, a fireplace and a folded up NordicTrack. Chalet style, the walls are steeply angled and near the top are three skylight windows. The walls and shelves are decorated with family photos, antique ski paraphernalia, tarnished sterling silver collectibles and expensive looking artifacts from around the world. Aside from the Jacuzzi, everything has been tastefully curated over generations. On one side of the room, close to the Jacuzzi, a frosted over sliding glass door, snow-covered pine trees faintly visible outside. On the other side, a door leading to the rest of the house. The phone onstage rings four times. House lights dim. The answering machine picks up.)

ANSWERING MACHINE. *(***JACKIE** *and* **ROBERT** *'s voices)* Hi, we're not here right now. *(***ROBERT** *'s voice)* At the message leave a beep. *(They laugh.)* BEEEP. *(***MAN** *'s voice)* Hi. This is Centennial Vacation Home Services. We got your message. So sorry about the situation with Helene Douglass. We haven't been able to get in touch with her either, but when we do, she will no longer be employed here. We're taking steps on our end to make sure something like this never happens again. Again, sorry. If you have a change of heart and would like to use us again in the future, we would love to make this right. Enjoy your time on the mountain. Sorry this is a long message.

(Lights onstage fade to black.)

Projection: Thursday

(A **WOMAN** *and a* **MAN** *sit in the Jacuzzi reading two identical copies of the parenting book "Making Bobby Robert" by Jackie and* **ROBERT ELDER**. *On the cover is a black and white photograph of a young boy. On a shelf behind the Jacuzzi is a bottle of brandy. The* **MAN** *has long straight hair, the* **WOMAN** *long wavy hair. Her arm is draped over the back of the tub.)*

(After a long stare:)

WOMAN. Why are you looking at me like that?

MAN. You look relaxed.

WOMAN. I am.

MAN. This is your calm face.

(She takes a deep inhale and smiles.)

WOMAN. I really like your hair long.

MAN. Thanks. Good week.

WOMAN. Yep.

(He goes back to reading. She points at the ceiling.)

I always love those things. With all…that kind of stuff and big, you know, what do you call those?

MAN. Yeah, I dunno. They're nice.

(They take in the room for a while.)

WOMAN. Have you seen my bag?

(He points to her backpack by the door.)

No my arm bag.

(She raises her arm up. There is a cast on it.)

MAN. Ah. I think it's in the shower. Want it?

WOMAN. Could you?

MAN. Yep.

WOMAN. Thank you.

(He gets out of the tub, shakes off the water, puts on a robe and crosses to the door. He passes the phone.)

MAN. There's a message.

(He exits.)

WOMAN. *(quietly)* Mm. Ah.

(She stares [towards the audience] at something on the wall in front of her. She does a little head tilt, interested. He returns with a plastic bag and puts it over her cast.)

Isn't it funny how the matting on that picture is the same color as the wall? Do you know what you could do? You could just put a frame up and then have a picture inside it, but the matting is actually the wall.

(They stare at the wall.)

MAN. Wait, I don't get it.

WOMAN. You have the frame up, with just that and that is actually just the wall.

MAN. Ohohohohohohohyeahyeahyeahyeahyeahyeah.

(They look at the picture.)

Yeah.

(He smiles. She looks at her arm.)

WOMAN. Thanks.

MAN. Yep.

(He goes to the answering machine.)

WOMAN. It's probably Centennial.

(presses play)

ANSWERING MACHINE. Hi. This is Centennial Vacation Home Services.

(They smile and make a "there ya go" gesture.)

We got your message. So sorry about the situation with Helene Douglass. We haven't been able to get in touch with her either, but when we do, she will no longer be employed here. /We're taking steps –

WOMAN. Great.

(He deletes the message. Second message plays.)

A MAN'S VOICE. Robert. Been a while. I hear you're back this weekend. Hey…you're a fuckin' piece of shit.

(They look at each other.)

WOMAN. Well, that's friendly.

MAN. Mr. Popular.

(He deletes the message. She turns on the TV.)

WOMAN. I wanna see what the weather's going to be like.

MAN. They said it's gonna be clear all weekend.

(She turns off the TV.)

Gotta get up early tomorrow.

(He takes off his robe.)

WOMAN. We'll go to bed soon. Did you burn the garbage?

MAN. Yeah.

(He dips a leg in.)

WOMAN. The bathroom garbage too?

MAN. Oh shit.

WOMAN. I can do it.

MAN. I can do it.

(He climbs back in the tub. Feels a twinge in his back.)

Ech. My back still hurts.

WOMAN. There's *every* kind of medicine in the cabinet.

MAN. Really?

WOMAN. Yeah…prescription stuff too.

MAN. Hm.

WOMAN. Yup.

MAN. I didn't even think about that stuff.

WOMAN. It's the first place I look. Do you know who I was just thinking of?

MAN. Grace?

WOMAN. Grace. Yeah.

(They smile. He goes back to reading.)

Did you get to the bedwetting section yet?

MAN. No.

WOMAN. It's really sad.

MAN. Don't ruin it.

WOMAN. It blew my mind.

(He keeps reading. She closes her eyes.)

There are pictures in the middle.

(He flips to the middle of the book.)

MAN. Wow. *(flips)* Wow. *(flip)* Whoa.

WOMAN. You're gonna get the cover wet.

MAN. There's a whole box of them in the closet. *(reading from the book)* "For one week we made sure to never laugh in front of Bobby. Anyone visiting our home wore cardboard masks, ensuring emotionally neutral expressions." That's a great picture.

(He shows her a page in the book.)

WOMAN. Yeah.

MAN. I would love to go back to Maine.

WOMAN. *(a little laugh)* We can't go back to Maine.

MAN. I know.

WOMAN. I mean, we could go –

(sound of a snowmobile pulling up)

Someone's home.

MAN. Yeah.

*(A tiny beat considering what to do… They go back to reading. The door slides open and **BO** enters the room wearing full neon ski gear and ski mask.)*

BO. Fuck! Uh – Oops. I'm so sorry.

> (**BO** *exits immediately, closing the door behind him. They look at each other blankly. The* **MAN** *turns on the bubbles.*)

WOMAN. Are you by a jet?

MAN. Yeah, back and foot.

WOMAN. Nice.

> (*Quiet knocking at the door. They look at each other. The knocking gets louder.*)

MAN. Come in.

> (**BO** *re-enters. He seems frazzled and a little tweaked out. He's carrying a big empty duffel bag.*)

BO. Hi, sorry… I'm – I'm just a little –

WOMAN. *(totally calm)* Can we help you?

BO. My dad is Robert Elder? Are you guys renting or –

WOMAN. Oh! Alright.

BO. Are you…he didn't tell me someone would be here.

MAN. Oh. Sorry.

BO. Nono… I wasn't supposed to come until tomorrow, so…

WOMAN. Yeah, sorry, he told us tomorrow.

BO. So you…sorry… I should've –

WOMAN. No.

BO. I…ah. It never really crossed my mind – don't wanna to barge in.

MAN. It's cool.

> (**BO** *leaves the door open, crosses past the Jacuzzi and looks around the room. The* **MAN** *turns off bubbles.*)

BO. Uh… Fuck!

WOMAN. Do you mind shutting the door?

BO. Sorry. *(getting more agitated)* I'll come back…early in the morning, I guess, is that ok? I don't know what the deal is.

MAN. Sure.

BO. Fucking Jacuzzi, that's crazy. *(He leans on the Jacuzzi, puts his head down and mutters to himself.)* OK, how the fuck's that gonna work. Fucking where am I gonna –. Fuck… *(He stands thinking for a second.)* Shit… *(trying to play it cool)* hey, is it ok if I leave some stuff –

WOMAN. Could you shut the door please?

BO. Fuck! Sorry.

> *(He crosses to the door and shuts it. He quietly leans his head against the wall.)*

WOMAN. Is it just you?

BO. Hm?

WOMAN. Is it just you tonight?

BO. *(He turns to face them, upset and seemingly near tears.)* Yeah, it's not much stuff, I just don't want to haul it all back down the mountain!

MAN. *(smiling)* Calm down man, it's all cool.

WOMAN. Take a minute, warm up.

BO. Yeah?

MAN. Of course.

BO. Yeah. *(beat)* Thanks, yeah.

WOMAN. What's your name?

BO. Oh… Bo.

WOMAN. I'm Helene and this is –

DEREK. Derek.

BO. Cool. Cool. When I came in I was like, whoa, wrong place. *(pointing to the Jacuzzi)* My dad must have just bought this fucker. Oh man. Thanks so much guys. You guys are great. *(pointing)* Helene. Derek?

HELENE.	**DEREK.**
Yep.	Yep.

BO. Bo. Thanks so much guys. It's just been a long day. What… *(thinking)* car, two planes, cab then renting the snowmobile.

HELENE. Did the wind pick up?

DEREK. We were saying it sounded rough out there.

BO. Yeah, yeah it got super windy coming up from the north side.

HELENE. Do you want some tea or hot cocoa?

BO. Nonono. Sorry, this is trippy for me. I just need a minute.

HELENE. Please, take your time.

> (**BO** *glances around the room.*)

BO. Hey…do you mind if I look around real quick?

HELENE. Go for it.

BO. This is so crazy. I haven't been here since I was a kid.

HELENE. Wow.

BO. Yeah.

> (*He takes his duffel bag and exits into the next room.*)

HELENE. This is great.

DEREK. *Helene.*

HELENE. Yeah?

> (*They smile.* **DEREK** *climbs out of the Jacuzzi. He quickly and quietly takes the two books and hides them in the bookshelf.*)

DEREK. Do you want me to –

HELENE. Just a second. (**HELENE** *in deep thought, then:*) OK, what?

DEREK. Do you think it's too hot in there?

HELENE. Mmm…feels / good.

> (*A crash from the kitchen.* **HELENE** *and* **DEREK** *look at each other. Beat.*)

BO. (*yelling from the other room*) Where you guys from?

DEREK. Originally?

BO. Yeah.

> (*During the following* **HELENE** *and* **DEREK** *don't break eye contact as they answer.*)

HELENE. Arizona.

DEREK. She's from Tucson. I'm from just outside Phoenix.

HELENE. We met in Flagstaff.

BO. Cool.

HELENE. You been?

BO. Where?

HELENE. Flagstaff.

BO. No I haven't.

HELENE. It's great.

BO. Could I have one of these colas?

HELENE. Help yourself to whatever you'd like.

DEREK. What's ours is yours man.

> (**DEREK** *gets back in the tub.* **BO** *enters with three cans of cola, duffel bag, now clearly full, slung over his shoulder.*)

BO. You want?

DEREK. Sure.

> (**BO** *drops the bag to the ground with a crash. Everyone chooses to ignore it.*)

HELENE. Thanks.

BO. What happened to your wrist?

HELENE. I just broke it.

> (*They open their cans.*)

BO. Are you left handed?

HELENE. No.

BO. I am. You're lucky, usually if you fall – you were skiing?

HELENE. Yeah.

BO. Mm-hm. Usually you put out your dominant hand to catch yourself, so you were lucky.

> (**HELENE** *sips.*)

HELENE. Ugh.

BO. What? *(sips)* Blech.

> (**DEREK** *takes a sip.*)

DEREK. Bah.

HELENE. It tastes like metal.

BO. These are fuckin' super old.

> (**DEREK** *holds out the brandy bottle.*)

DEREK. This helps.

BO. What do you got there, buddy?

DEREK. Brandy.

BO. No thanks. Well. Maybe just a tiny little nip nip.

> (**DEREK** *passes the bottle to* **BO.** **BO** *pours brandy into his mouth, making sure his lips don't touch the bottle.*)

Hiker's pour.

HELENE. You should stay.

BO. What?

HELENE. You should totally stay here. I mean if you want. *(looks at* **DEREK***)* Right?

DEREK. Oh yeah, of course.

BO. No…

DEREK. Yeah, of course. If you don't mind us being here. We're going to bed soon. I mean –

BO. No.

DEREK. Honestly. We don't care one way or another. Please…you're very welcome to stay. There's plenty of room… Sorry for the confusion.

BO. No. Dude not at all. I should have called. I wasn't gonna come and then last minute I was like I was gonna come. I don't wanna ruin your vacation.

DEREK. Pff. Not at all.

HELENE. Pff.

BO. Um…fuck. Thanks guys. Maybe for a little bit.

DEREK. Of course.

BO. *(Drinks. Smiles. Finally letting down his guard a bit, but trembling a little.)* This is hitting the spot. Great place, huh? You guys big skiers?

HELENE. Not really. We just like this area.

> (**BO** *discreetly takes a pill.*)

BO. Yeah, it's beautiful. Great time of year to be here. You been here for Rendezvous weekend before?

HELENE. No.

BO. Altitude get to you?

DEREK. At first, but now we're cool.

BO. *(trembling again)* Oof. I'm fucking freezing…do you mind?

DEREK. Hop in man.

HELENE. Come on in.

> (**BO** *strips down to his underwear as* **HELENE** *and* **DEREK** *watch, amused.* **HELENE** *leans forward on the edge of the tub, slightly predatorily.* **BO** *walks towards the tub, then stops himself.*)

BO. Is that weird?

DEREK & HELENE. No.

> *(Lights dim.)*

> *(Transition:* **DEREK** *gets out of the Jacuzzi.* **BO** *gets in the Jacuzzi with* **HELENE**. *He drinks from the brandy bottle. He's getting tipsy. Lights back up.* **DEREK** *stands outside peeing on the deck, bare ass visible through the frosty glass.)*

BO. He…just pees right there?

HELENE. He doesn't like peeing inside.

BO. That's cool. I like that. Breaking something on vacation sucks, right?

HELENE. It was a clean break. So that's good.

BO. Sweet. Did you know that you can't break a bone in the exact same place twice?

HELENE. Are you sure?

BO. Yeah totally. You and tall guy. Are you guys married or…

HELENE. No.

BO. But you guys are like a thing, right?

HELENE. Yeah, we're a thing.

BO. My parents were really into weird sex here.

HELENE. Oh yeah?

> (**DEREK** *returns and climbs back into the Jacuzzi.*)

BO. OH yeah. Like freaks back in the day. And now they want to kill each other. My mom lost a lot of weight around the divorce and then my Dad wanted to get back together. They brought that up in court it was really messed up. Now she's fat again. You guys check out my sweet gear when I came in?

DEREK. No.

HELENE. No.

BO. Dad and me are doing the Rendezvous Father/Son fucking race. Thought I'd at least look cool. Picked up all this new gear in Switzerland. Rad colors. No one has anything like it here. I don't even know if it's out yet or they sell it here. Crazy expensive.

> (**BO** *takes a huge slug of brandy.*)

DEREK. You travel a lot?

BO. It's like all I do!

DEREK. I was in Belize last fall.

HELENE. He loves to travel.

DEREK. So does she.

BO. Cool. Yeah, I did Ayuda in Nicaragua in high school. My girlfriend was really into that stuff. They wanted me to build toilets and shit. (**HELENE** *and* **DEREK** *start laughing,* **BO** *continues as if it's an awesome joke.*) I called my parents and was like this is hell my girlfriend is covered in shit and being all cold and drinking with old Mexican guys get me the fuck out of here.

> (**HELENE** *and* **DEREK** *laugh so hard, slapping the water. Their laughter fades as they watch* **BO** *pound the brandy.*)

This is kicked. Guys I know where the good stuff is or where it used to be.

> (**BO** *climbs out of the Jacuzzi, and towel-less hustles through the cold living room to the door.*)

Wooo! Wooooo!

> (*He exits.*)

HELENE. I don't want to go to bed now.

DEREK. Fun.

HELENE. Derek…?

DEREK. Yep.

> (**BO** *enters with a bottle of wine.*)

BO. Boom. This is from France. My mom would shove these in her luggage and then hide them in her bathroom.

> (**BO** *splashes back into the tub.*)

How 'bout Argentina? You been there?

DEREK. No.

BO. It's wild. You can ride wild Clydesdales.

HELENE. Are you an only child?

BO. I have a brother actually. He's older with kids. I never see him.

HELENE. No sisters.

BO. No sisters. You?

HELENE. He's from a family of eight kids and I'm from a family of ten kids.

BO. No.

> (*They look at each other then rattle off names SO quickly.*)

HELENE. JeanJennyBradyJoeJaySueHeleneMarkMarcyJohn

DEREK. PamHopeDerekBryceDavidBossyShaunLacy.

BO. Whoa.

DEREK. Yep, big families.

HELENE. Do you remember the show about that big family – Wait, how old are you?

BO. I'm twenty-six. How old are you?

DEREK. She won't tell you. See if you can get her to tell you. I don't think she'll tell you. I'm forty-four.

BO. No!

DEREK. No. I'm thirty-six.

BO. Helene.

HELENE. Bo.

BO. How old are you?

HELENE. Nope.

BO. I'm gonna guess.

HELENE. OK.

BO. Thirty.

HELENE. Yep. Thirty.

> (**BO** *chugs.*)

BO. Fuck! My dad's coming tomorrow. That's just so weird. I haven't seen him in since a long time.

HELENE. Why's that?

BO. Just shitty you know, basically divorce stuff. They waited 'til I left for college to get divorced. And then –

DEREK. Where did you go to school?

BO. High school?

DEREK. College.

BO. I went to Briarly for high school. And then different places for college.

DEREK. So you left for college –

BO. Yeah, and then they got divorced and man, you know, they were fighting over this place and then my fucking dad – *(He stops cold and looks at* **HELENE** *and* **DEREK**, *suddenly a touch paranoid)…* Wait, you know my dad. Do you know my dad?

HELENE. No, just from the phone and stuff. I don't really know him…just setting things up on the phone.

BO. Rightright. *(looking at* **HELENE***)* My grandma had that swimsuit. (**DEREK** *and* **HELENE** *shoot a quick glance.*) My parents did some fucked up things to us. My mom hit me once with a belt. Stuff like that. *That's* not in their book. My dad used all that so he could get what he wanted in court. *(beat)* I'm so much like my mother it's fucking crazy.

HELENE. Wow.

BO. Yeah. *(beat)* This place is from railroad days.

DEREK. Wow.

BO. Yeah.

You wanna hear something really fucked up? **(HELENE** *nods.)* My dad is paying me to visit him. Man that's sad. Your parents married?

DEREK. Yeah.

HELENE. Yeah.

BO. Awesome. Wow that's great. No one's is anymore.

> *(***DEREK*** *touches* **BO***'s shoulder.)*

DEREK. It's alright buddy.

BO. *(trying to keep from crying)* Yeah. *(smiling)* You guys are awesome. In France I dated this crazy older woman who was like thirty-five and she did something really fucking bad to be with me. Like she wanted to marry me and shit… I didn't know she had a fuckin' little kid…ugh so fucking sad man… Not my fault…this is not the time to share this. Ahhh… I trust you guys though, you don't know her. Shit got so messed up. I left her and she followed me. Helene you have a lot of hair.

HELENE. Thanks.

BO. You get that a lot?

HELENE. Sometimes. I change it a lot.

BO. I like all type of women. You got a type brother?

DEREK. I have weird taste.

HELENE. He likes girls that like him.

DEREK. Or that really don't like me. I love that.

BO. I don't get it.

(**BO** *leans in to kiss* **HELENE**. **DEREK** *pulls his head back.*)

BO. *(getting super dark. Starting to cry a bit)* I did something bad in Romamia, I don't wanna tell you about it. Maybe I should tell you about it. I fucked up, man.

(**BO** *slips underwater.* **HELENE** *and* **DEREK** *look at each other, amused. He's staying down. For a while. Their faces drop. Is he ok? He re-emerges.*)

I gotta get my shit together. *(Getting even darker and quieter. Totally lost.)* She showed up with her fucking kid in fucking Romamia and she started at me. She wouldn't quit. I fucking pushed her so fucking hard. I think I'm going to get in trouble for that. My dad is paying me to be here. How sad is that? Do you think I'm going to get in trouble for that?

DEREK. Hm.

BO. Do you know what? I was just gonna take my all this shit and go. Steal this fucker's – all this shit.

HELENE. Like what?

BO. *(angrily)* This shit is worth so much money. So much money. *(pointing)* The fucking thingy thing. My mom's fucking folk arts and crap. Yeah. *(pointing)* Even the fucking handles, those metal handles are designed by some guy.

HELENE. That's ok.

DEREK. Parent stuff is hard.

HELENE. Yeah.

(**BO** *stares. He leans in and smells* **HELENE**'s *hair. He falls into her, sniffing, whimpering, breathing deep.* **HELENE** *and* **DEREK** *look at each other blankly.* **DEREK** *suddenly, violently pulls* **BO** *back by his hair and pins him against the side of the Jacuzzi.*)

DEREK. It's ok man.

HELENE. Let's get him outta here.

(**HELENE** *climbs out.* **DEREK** *begins pulling* **BO** *out.*)

HELENE. I'm glad that we were here.

BO. Me too.

I always make a mess, man.

(**BO** *stumbles, trying to pick up his clothes.* **HELENE** *leads him out of the room.* **DEREK** *follows, picking up the duffel and the rest of* **BO**'*s things.* **DEREK** *looks the room over and flicks off the light.*)

HELENE. *(voice over)* Ahh, Colorado. I love to get away. The past few weeks had been really really nice. Reconnecting with each other. And this house. Wow. I'm so glad we picked this house. So many home movies. Cassette tapes. Journals. Books. Art projects. Manuscripts. Scrapbooks. Prescriptions. Keepsakes. Photo albums. Letters. Clothes. Undergarments. Still…it was nice to have some company.

Projection: Friday

(The next morning. The house is spotless. Cinematic '80s synth rock blasts. Sound of a helicopter arriving and hovering. A face peers through the frosted glass. **ROBERT** *opens the sliding door, then turns to wave as the helicopter roars off. He enters, headphones on, brushes the snow off his new Ralph Lauren parka and sets down his leather duffel bag. He looks at the Jacuzzi and smiles. He walks past it, triumphantly swiping a handful of water into the air. He stands, staring at the tub.* **HELENE** *enters behind him. She looks different. Maybe wearing a man's flannel shirt and ripped Levis.)*

HELENE. Hi Mr. Elder. *(He doesn't hear.)* Mr. Elder!

ROBERT. Oh!

*(***ROBERT*** wheels around and pulls off his headphones, the music drops low, just coming through the headphones now.)*

HELENE. How was your flight?

ROBERT. Good. Good.

*(***ROBERT*** turns off his Walkman.)*

HELENE. Lucked out with weather. Bo's here. He's sleeping.

ROBERT. What?

*(***HELENE*** *is super peppy,* ***ROBERT*** *is very confused.)*

HELENE. Bo got here last night. He came in early. It was nice to meet him.

ROBERT. OK… I – I'm…sorry. Who the hell are you?

HELENE. Oh. Oh my God. I'm sorry. *(laughs for a little too long)* I'm Helene.

ROBERT. Oh! Helene!

HELENE. I'm so sorry, I thought you knew I'd be here.

ROBERT. I didn't know that you'd *be here* be here.

HELENE. Oh.

ROBERT. Sorry I didn't immediately – Bo's here you say?

HELENE. Yep. I think he wanted to surprise you.

ROBERT. Hm… Wow. He came. Alright.

> (**ROBERT** *takes in the room.*)

Helene. It looks great. You really… And this guy *(pointing at the Jacuzzi)* …oh dear lord. Yeah. Fuck you, Jackie. Fuuuuuck you. Her father would just die if he saw this in here. We couldn't even wear shoes in this house. This is great. How'd they get it in? They take the doors off?

HELENE. That's usually what they have to do.

ROBERT. Wow. *(pointing at one of the skylights)* And that's the window we had replaced?

HELENE. Mm-hm.

ROBERT. Really?

HELENE. Yep. *(taking it in)* That's the one.

ROBERT. Wow. I wouldn't even – yeah, it looks great.

HELENE. Yeah, they do nice work.

ROBERT. They sure do.

> (**DEREK** *enters, unseen, stands right behind* **ROBERT**, *and joins* **ROBERT** *and* **HELENE** *in looking up at the window.* **ROBERT** *feels his presence and turns.*)

Hello.

DEREK. Hi.

ROBERT. Are you the muscle in this operation?

> (**DEREK** *looks past* **ROBERT** *at* **HELENE**, *who smiles.*)

DEREK. Guess so. Hi Mr. Elder. I'm Derek.

ROBERT. Please guys, call me Robert.

DEREK. Good to meet you Robert.

ROBERT. Good to meet you Erik. *("ERIK" and* **HELENE** *register* **ROBERT***'s mistake.)* Thank you for everything you did. The place looks great.

ERIK. Oh no, I didn't do anything.

HELENE. *Erik,* grab his bags.

ROBERT. That's all I have. I travel light these days. Got it down to one bag.

ERIK. I'll grab it.

ROBERT. Don't worry about it.

ERIK. I got it.

(**ERIK** *exits with* **ROBERT***'s bag.)*

ROBERT. Man, this is… Fuck you Jackie.

HELENE. Jackie sent some fruit.

ROBERT. *(suddenly serious)* She did? Really? What's that about?

HELENE. Grapefruits. They're on the kitchen counter. There's a note.

ROBERT. She's doing something… I'm not gonna think about it. Where's Bo?

HELENE. He's still sleeping. Had a rough night.

ROBERT. Wait…you were here last night?

HELENE. Yep.

(beat)

ROBERT. …You didn't let him drink did you?

HELENE. No.

ROBERT. Hm. Ha. This place.

(**ROBERT** *crosses to the door.* **ERIK** *re-enters.)*

ERIK. I put it in the master bedroom.

ROBERT. Great!

(**ROBERT** *wanders off through the house.* **ERIK** *and* **HELENE** *stand there smiling.* **ROBERT** *returns. He walks to the Jacuzzi.)*

So what do I need to know about this thing?

ERIK. She's all set for ya.

ROBERT. I tell ya… I'm sorry, I'm just gonna hop right in this thing. That ok?

HELENE. Of course.

ERIK. *(points to a button)* Bubbles right there.

ROBERT. Gotcha. Thanks again for everything.

> *(**ROBERT** begins quickly stripping down to his boxer shorts.)*

HELENE. Enjoy. We're gonna finish packing up our tools and head out in, what – about an hour?

ERIK. Hour and a half.

ROBERT. Good, I'm looking forward to some alone time with my son.

> *(**ROBERT** starts easing into the Jacuzzi. He's in heaven. Ooohing and splashing, not really paying too much attention to what **HELENE** is saying.)*

HELENE. I just finished caulking the kitchen sink, which had a leak. Few other things on my list Erik couldn't get to. There are some branches down from last night so we'll clear your trail. Um, let's see…is there anything you were wondering about?

ROBERT. MCI is switched on?

> *(**HELENE** turns to **ERIK**.)*

ERIK. Yeah, phone should be good.

> *(**ROBERT** stands up and starts scanning the room.)*

HELENE. What do you need?

ROBERT. The clicker.

> *(**ERIK** picks up the remote but before he can hand it to **ROBERT**:)*

HELENE. Oh yeah. Shit. Erik?

ERIK. Oh. Satellite's not responding yet, don't really know why, could just be the cold.

ROBERT. No!

HELENE. Erik's really good at that stuff, he'll take a look at that.

> *(While she talks,* **ERIK** *walks to the TV, yanks out a cable from the back, and pockets it.)*

And then before we leave we can show you the ratio of chemicals to add to the water and bacteria checks and pH levels. All that stuff.

ROBERT. Oh. Is this…a lot of up keep?

HELENE. Not really but, well – a fair amount yeah.

> *(They laugh.* **HELENE**'s *delightful and* **ROBERT** *is eating it up.)*

ERIK. It's easy to learn.

> *(***ERIK** *exits out the sliding door.)*

HELENE. OK. Enjoy!

ROBERT. I will.

> *(***HELENE** *exits.* **ROBERT** *stands in the middle of the water. He slowly turns and takes in the room. He sits down in the water. He is gleaming with happiness.* **HELENE** *enters quietly with towels.)*

HELENE. *(whispers)* Sorry. I'm just gonna put these right here.

ROBERT. Hm?

HELENE. *(louder)* I'm just gonna put these right here.

ROBERT. No problem. This is really incredible. I'm in a Jacuzzi.

HELENE. Enjoy.

> *(***HELENE** *smiles and starts to leave.)*

ROBERT. Do you know how to turn on the stereo?

HELENE. Oh, let's see. I can figure it out.

ROBERT. Can you put something on?

HELENE. You got it!

ROBERT. *(repeating)* "You got it!" You are so easy going. I like that. What do you like to listen to?

HELENE. I like everything.

> (**HELENE** *takes a tape out of the cassette player and slips it in her pocket.*)

ROBERT. You pick. Something classical though. From the bottom shelf. Gotta get some firewood. What happened to your arm?

HELENE. Landed weird.

ROBERT. Ouch.

HELENE. Yeah.

ROBERT. Kid still sleepin, huh?

HELENE. I guess so.

> (**HELENE** *puts in a tape. It's very loud.*)

ROBERT. Hello!

HELENE. Oops sorry.

> (*She turns the volume down.*)

ROBERT. This is nice. What's this?

HELENE. It's a compilation… *(reading)* "Live at Ravinia."

ROBERT. Oh, no…that's a big concert place Jackie's family contributes to. Change this, it's upsetting.

> (**HELENE** *finds another tape. She starts it.*)

Now this is good. Oh yeah. Here we go.

> (**ROBERT** *takes a deep breath almost about to finally relax.* **HELENE** *takes this as a sign to exit. The phone rings.*)

Shit. Helene? Can you?

HELENE. Of course.

> (*She returns.*)

ROBERT. You know what, no. Let the machine take it.

> (*The answering machine clicks.*)

ANSWERING MACHINE. Hey, we're not here right now / at the message leave a beep. *(laugh)*

ROBERT. *(quietly)* Oh God.

> (**ROBERT** *puts his head in his hands, listening to himself and Jackie on the outgoing message. Machine beeps.*)

A WOMAN'S VOICE. Hiya Robert, don't know if you've made it in yet. It's Cassie, no rush, just some updated tour stops and signings. Ring me up if you want. Enjoy your weekend.

> (**ROBERT** *sits up.*)

ROBERT. I have to change that message.

HELENE. Do you want me to erase this?

ROBERT. No. Actually can you just redo the outgoing message?

HELENE. I... OK.

ROBERT. Just say we aren't home. In a nice way. That will throw Jackie for a loop.

> (**HELENE** *begins to record.*)

HELENE. *(sexy)* Hi we're not here right now. At the message leave us a beep. *(girlish giggle)*

> (**ROBERT** *smiles and points at* **HELENE.**)

ROBERT. Good. Very good. Man this thing gets hot. Do you know how to turn the temp down a little?

HELENE. Sure. *(turns it down).* Got it. It's right here.

ROBERT. Oh man. Finally. For *years...* I've been like: This place needs a Jacuzzi. You have no idea the things I now know about divorce and Colorado property law. You don't *wanna* know the things I know about Colorado property laws. The things I could tell you... Do you have receipts for all the stuff?

HELENE. *(She points to his chest.)* What's that? I'm sorry.

ROBERT. It's alright. Pacemaker.

HELENE. Should you be in a Jacuzzi?

ROBERT. Totally safe.

HELENE. Does it beep at the airport?

ROBERT. Yep.

> *(They laugh.* **BO** *enters.* **ROBERT** *stands.)*

Son.

BO. Dad.

> *(***ROBERT** *gets out of the tub. He slowly walks towards* **BO** *who looks very uncomfortable.* **HELENE** *takes a towel, gets on her hands and knees and mops up the floor behind him.* **ROBERT** *goes in to give* **BO** *a wet hug.)*

Dad. You're wet.

ROBERT. Jesus, you look fantastic Bobby.

BO. Bo.

ROBERT. You gotta stay at this weight.

BO. *(quietly)* Oh god.

ROBERT. Bobby, I can see you are being healthy.

> *(***BO** *looks at* **HELENE** *cleaning the floor. A little confused.)*

BO. Wait. Why are you still here?

HELENE. We're just clearing the trail and we want to get some other stuff taken care of.

BO. What? Don't worry about that we'll call someone.

> *(***BO** *takes the towel from* **HELENE**.*)*

HELENE. No, that's fine.

BO. Dad!

ROBERT. What?

BO. Why are you making them do work for you?

ROBERT. What?

BO. Call someone to do the trail work.

ROBERT. Uh…hello! She does it all. They do it all.

HELENE. Yeah.

BO. Oh! Wait…huh? I'm sorry…

ROBERT. I tell ya… They. Are. Top. Notch. Especially this
     one.

HELENE. Thanks.

BO. Waitwait, you…

> (**HELENE** *just smiles.*)

…you work here?

ROBERT. Yeah.

BO. Oh. God. Sorry, I didn't mean to… I thought that
     you were like *staying* here. *(beat)* Renting. *(beat)* I don't
     know why I thought that.

> (**HELENE** *takes the towel back from* **BO**.)

HELENE. Nope, just last night to test the Jacuzzi. Oh! The
     receipts. I'll grab those right now.

> (**HELENE** *exits.* **ROBERT** *and* **BO** *stand quietly for
> a bit.*)

ROBERT. Man, you look like…

BO. What?

ROBERT. Just…good to see you. You look older.

BO. I am older.

ROBERT. Does your mom know you're here?

BO. Nope. We aren't talking. Haven't in months.

ROBERT. Well, I'm glad you came.

BO. Coolcool. Well.

ROBERT. Wasn't sure you would. You look great.

BO. You too.

ROBERT. You bring your skis?

BO. I don't know where they are. We should get me some
     new ones.

ROBERT. Great.

> (*They stand quietly for a bit.* **HELENE** *returns with
> a list.*)

How's it coming Helene?

HELENE. Good.

ROBERT. Helene's so great.

BO. Yeah?

HELENE. Stop it! Alright… Let's see…

> *(She jots down a couple numbers on the top of the list)*

So here's the total…that's for, you know the sink, trail maintenance, all that. We do itemized lists instead of individual receipts now.

ROBERT. Oh. And what is it for the rest? For you and Erik?

BO. Derek, dad.

HELENE. It's Erik. Eh, we can take care of that later.

ROBERT. Is a check ok?

HELENE. Oh. Um. Yyyeah. Yeahyeah.

ROBERT. Yeah, let's do cash.

HELENE. Either way.

ROBERT. It's fine. I brought a ton of cash.

> *(**ROBERT** exits.)*

BO. I didn't mean to be offensive or anything before. About the whole working thing.

HELENE. Not at all.

BO. I had an internship once, so… Fun time last night.

HELENE. Yeah, right?

BO. *(playing it cool but feeling her out)* You hung over?

HELENE. Nope.

BO. My head is throbbing. Did I…say…anything…stupid… shit?

HELENE. Mm… I don't think so… Uuuuuh… No.

BO. Cool.

HELENE. Hope you enjoy your time here. We'll be bopping in and – popping. Sorry my mom says bopping, we'll be *popping* in and out I'm sure.

BO. Oh cool. Good.

HELENE. Clearing the branches from the trail…

(**ROBERT** *returns in a robe with cash, a pamphlet and floss.*)

ROBERT. Thank you. (*He hands a large wad of cash to* **HELENE**.)

HELENE. Thanks.

(**ROBERT** *walks to* **BO**, *gives him a few bills.*)

BO. (*upset*) Wait –

ROBERT. You'll get the rest after the race.

BO. So. You finally got your Jacuzzi.

ROBERT. I had them put it right in the middle of the floor so it would cover up your peepee / stain.

BO. Dad.

ROBERT. (*laughing*) I'm sorry, I'm sorry.

I forget what he had. Some kind of kidney issue because…it just turned that wood BLACK.

BO. (*quietly*) Oh my God.

(*The guys stand quietly for a while, taking in the room.* **ROBERT** *pulls out a piece of floss and starts flossing.*)

ROBERT. I used to chain smoke and my hypnotherapist who helped me quit recommended flossing.

HELENE. Cool. Excuse me, I gotta finish up that stuff.

ROBERT. Thanks Helene.

(**HELENE** *exits.* **ROBERT** *finishes flossing and drops the floss on the floor. He looks at the pamphlet.*)

Here, we should go over this, it has this year's race route. And all the fun food stands we pass.

BO. I'll just follow you.

ROBERT. Come on, get into it!

BO. I thought the Bancrofts still kept this place up.

ROBERT. They did. They were very close with your mother's family. And I didn't want to put myself in the middle of all that. So I started going through some company.

(**BO** *sits in front of the fireplace and counts his money.*)

BO. Mom's fucking Jim Michael Dean again.

ROBERT. I'm eating.

BO. I just heard that from Jim's daughter who was in Prague for one night.

ROBERT. I don't care.

BO. Alright.

> (*tiny beat*)

ROBERT. How long? Have they been back together?

BO. I don't know we aren't talking.

ROBERT. But you know they're screwing…

BO. Yup, Jim's daughter was pissed 'cause her mom found out.

ROBERT. Yeah, I don't care.

> (*beat*)

Jim still…acting?

BO. He's on that cop show. As like the main guy.

ROBERT. I don't care.

BO. Mom had said you finished your book.

ROBERT. Did she finish hers?

BO. I think so. It's been done since last summer. I know she finished up cover quotes.

ROBERT. Who did she ask?

BO. I don't remember…maybe Dr. Ron from TV.

ROBERT. Pff.

BO. And I don't fuckin' remember.

ROBERT. You should read mine while you're here. I have galleys.

BO. I'm not reading a diet book Dad.

ROBERT. It's more than that Bobby.

BO. Bo.

ROBERT. Sorry. How was Croatia?

(**BO** *stands.*)

BO. That was three years ago.

ROBERT. Right.

BO. I was in Pari/s.

(*He starts walking towards the door*)

ROBERT. Paris.

BO. I got fucking stuck. Remember?

ROBERT. Your mother said –

BO. She was not helpful either.

(**BO** *exits towards his room.*)

ROBERT. *(yelling)* Take you out for breakfast and ski shopping?

(*no answer*)

(yelling) One o'clock?

(*no answer*)

Sounds good.

(**ROBERT** *stretches his shoulder. He walks to the TV, picks up the remote and turns on the TV. Static. Turns it off.* **HELENE** *enters with hot tub chemicals. She spots the floss on the floor and throws it away.* **ROBERT** *looks around the room for a long time.*)

Oh boy. I gotta get all of Jackie's fucking crap out of here by Monday. Pack it up and ship it to her and her shitty brother. That's somehow my responsibility. Not complaining about that...happy about the way things...

HELENE. Yeah, that will change the energy in here. Getting it out.

ROBERT. Right?!

(**ROBERT** *pulls a frame off the wall.*)

God, I've always hated this painting.

HELENE. Yeah, it's pretty ugly. Sorry.

ROBERT. I don't care. This guy did those two too.

(**ROBERT** *stops, looks around the room again. There's so much shit. He walks to a cabinet and opens a draw full of junk.*)

ROBERT. *(under his breath)* Fuck me.

HELENE. Do you want a hand?

ROBERT. No thanks.

HELENE. You sure?

ROBERT. No thanks.

HELENE. Seriously, I'm happy to help. I actually used to work as a –

ROBERT. No thanks! Sorry. It's personal stuff. I'd rather take some time and look through it all by myself.

HELENE. Of course. Yeah.

(**ROBERT** *stops and smiles at* **HELENE.**)

ROBERT. Helene, your thing is that you need to be able to fix everything, to provide a solution. You're a Mender.

HELENE. Oh yeah? That's my thing?

ROBERT. Well…isn't it?

HELENE. Hm. Yeah, maybe. Let me think on it.

(**BO**, *dressed in ski garb, enters and crosses towards the sliding door.*)

ROBERT. That's a nice snowsuit. Are any of your old buddies on the mountain while you're here?

BO. I don't want to see anyone.

(**BO** *exits out the sliding door. He disappears out of view. We hear his snowmobile starting and then him driving away.*)

HELENE. What does Bo do?

ROBERT. What does Bo do? Ahhh…he's between things right now. He was doing some kind of teaching on a ship for a while. There's SO much shit.

HELENE. Yeah. There's a lot of stuff in this house.

ROBERT. Jackie was a very messy woman.

HELENE. How do you know what goes to her?

ROBERT. Uh...there's a list. All her family's stuff. Anything that's her family's. Most of the stuff that was ours together.

(**ERIK** *enters from outside.*)

ERIK. Hey man.

ROBERT. Hello.

HELENE. Where's the list?

ROBERT. It's in my bag.

(**HELENE** *exits to get the list.* **ROBERT** *pulls some snowshoes down off the wall, the shadow of their shape remains on the wall.* **ERIK** *turns on the TV. Static.*)

ERIK. Nope.

(**ERIK** *turns down the volume and then turns off the TV.* **ROBERT** *admires the show shoes.*)

Those are cool.

ROBERT. Always wanted to try these. They were always off limits because they're collectors' items.

(**HELENE** *enters with the list.*)

ERIK. They're really fun. I love getting out on the snow in those.

HELENE. Oh I love those!

ERIK. You know what I'm going to do? Re-angle the satellite dish.

HELENE. Hey Erik, all this stuff needs to get packed by Monday.

ERIK. *(taking in the room)* Oh wow. That's a big job.

HELENE. *(smiling)* Yeah.

(*Lights dim. Transition:* **ERIK** *and* **HELENE** *start packing.*)

Friday Afternoon

(The day passes. Late afternoon. Snowmobile engine idles outside. **HELENE** *is sorting and packing.* **BO** *sits staring at her.)*

BO. Hey if you find any jewelry my mom said I could have it.

HELENE. …OK I'll let you know.

(The snowmobile engine shuts off. **BO** *watches her sort for a while.)*

BO. How much is he paying you to sort all our stuff?

HELENE. I'm just doing it.

BO. Do you do this kind of thing a lot?

HELENE. Yeah, things like this.

BO. Is it weird to go through people's personal stuff.

HELENE. Um…no.

*(***ERIK*** *pops his head in the door.)*

ERIK. Hey Bo… Were you having any problems with the snowmobile?

BO. Uh…no.

ERIK. Huh. It's… I'm trying to move it off the path and it's not – …the idle didn't sound a little high to you?

BO. *(pretending to know)* Uh. Yeah. Yeah, it was a little high.

*(***ROBERT*** *snowshoes up to the sliding door.)*

ERIK. That's what I thought. Thanks.

BO. Don't use up the gas. I wanna ride down to town again later.

ERIK. We'll see if I can get it going man. Helene, what time is it?

HELENE. Quarter 'til.

ERIK. 'Til…

HELENE. Four.

ROBERT. Behind you!

ERIK. Op. Excuse me.

ROBERT. This is what they call a Rocky Mountain traffic jam.

ERIK. That's right.

> *(They awkwardly make their way past each other.* **ERIK** *walks off towards the snowmobile.* **ROBERT** *takes off the snowshoes and enters.)*

ROBERT. Mm. Good air out there. That was a nice recharge. Mm. I shoed up to where they're marking out the course for Sunday...comes, oh within maybe, eighth of a mile of here? A little out of breath there for a while cuz of the thin air. I saw a bird that just knocked my socks off. I'm gonna look it up in one of those nature books. *(grabs his hamstrings)* Geez, you really feel it right *here* with those don't you? *(taking in the room)* Wowie, you really made a dent in here.

HELENE. Thanks! I just started stacking boxes over in that corner and then a couple in the kitchen. Her list is pretty much everything.

ROBERT. Helene...here...smell this.

> *(***ROBERT** *hands* **HELENE** *a pine branch.)*

HELENE. Mmm. Yeah. I just checked in with Erik. We're a little behind. We'll come back first thing in the morning. Still need to put more hay around the pipes...

ROBERT. How about the satellite?

HELENE. Oy...

ROBERT. Couldn't get it to work?

HELENE. Not yet.

ROBERT. Formula 1 is on this weekend, so if he could try to have it done by then...

BO. Yeah, I want to watch that.

ROBERT. *(To* **BO**. *Measured.)* How was your day?

BO. Well. I went to town.

ROBERT. Fun!

BO. They fucking hate us.

ROBERT. What?

BO. I tried to get skis, gloves, and like *real* food at the trading post and when they realized who I was they were dicks. They wouldn't do credit.

ROBERT. That's crazy. Ed and Jean? What about cash? They wouldn't take cash?

BO. I didn't want to spend that cash. Ed was so fucking cold.

ROBERT. I'm sure you're being over sensitive. I'll call them. Helene, look up the number for the Trading Post.

BO. It's on their pencil.

> (**BO** *points to a pencil next to the telephone.* **ROBERT** *crosses to the phone, picks up the pencil and dials.*)

ROBERT. Hiya Buddy, it's *(in funny deep voice)* BIG BEAR BOOZER…*(normal voice)* Big Bear Boozer… Ed it's Robert Elder… Robert – …Yeah. Just got in this morning, wanted to say hello and we're doing Rocky Mountain Rendezvous – you what?… Huh?… Oh?… Well yeah… Yes, Bobby said you – uh uh…yeah… I did…well I'm… – that's a little harsh wouldn't you – OK buddy – *(Beat. Hangs up the phone with a fake smile.)*

BO. I'll wear Kevin's old yellow skis. Fuck it.

ROBERT. *(to* **HELENE***)* Jackie's family, they've been – I should say they *were*, her parents aren't with us anymore, *were* a bigbig family around here.

HELENE. Oh wow.

ROBERT. You know Marshall Peak?

HELENE. Sure.

ROBERT. *That's* Jackie's family.

HELENE. Oh wow. Wow.

BO. And now everyone hates us.

ROBERT. Stop it. Helene, did you know, this is interesting, this was originally a comfort station.

BO. Then grandpa paid someone off and got some European to design the shit out of this place.

ROBERT. Yep. Lot of history to this place. The beams are from the silver rush.

BO. That's not true.

ROBERT. Well…whatever.

HELENE. What do you need? We can just hop on the snowmobile and get you stuff in town.

ROBERT. What? No.

HELENE. Sure. Just make me a list.

ROBERT. We're fine.

HELENE. You wanna be comfortable. Here, I'll make it easy: snacks, drinks, paper towels, TP, beer, milk, hot chocolate…

BO. Some nice gloves. Socks. SPF. Gum. Jello.

ROBERT. Floss. Tonic!

HELENE. Alright!

> (**ERIK** *returns from outside and warms his hands in the Jacuzzi water.*)

ERIK. Sorry Bo. I don't know. I think the starter's just totally shot. Can't move it.

BO. Fuck.

HELENE. You wanna try again?

ERIK. It's totally shot.

ROBERT. Don't worry about it, Helene. We have cereal.

BO. I'm not eating cereal for dinner.

HELENE. *(She smiles at him.)* I bet you can get it.

ERIK. Yeah?

HELENE. Yeah. You're good at that stuff.

ERIK. Yeah. I'll give it another try.

ROBERT. If you can't get it I can call and have them switch it out.

ERIK. They're closed.

> (**ERIK** *exits.*)

ROBERT. Well…shit.

HELENE. Erik will get it. OK, what do you guys like to eat?

BO. For food?

HELENE. Yep.

BO. I dunno. Just get good stuff.

HELENE. Gotcha.

(*The snowmobile fires up.*)

ROBERT. Yeah!

HELENE. See! He's so good at that stuff. (*putting on her coat and boots*) So: (*quickly*) Snacks, drinks, paper towels, TP, beer, milk, hot chocolate, nice gloves, socks, SPF, gum, Jello, floss, tonic and good food. (*brightly*) Anything else?

ROBERT. Ha! Here.

(*He hands her some bills.*)

HELENE. Alright, see ya in a bit.

ROBERT. Alright.

(**HELENE** *exits.* **ROBERT** *watches her go.* **BO** *exits the room and heads to his bedroom.* **ROBERT** *doesn't notice.*)

That was nice. Good kids. Oh, I shoulda told them to get marshmallows. For s'mores! Get a big fire going! That'd be fun. But I guess we're not eating that stuff.

(*He turns around. Notices* **BO** *is gone. Lights out.*)

Friday Night

(BO and ROBERT sit quietly. ROBERT reads a nature book while BO plays with an old box of blocks.)

ROBERT. Hungry?

BO. Why?

ROBERT. Because it's dinner time... Because I'm going to make something nice when Helene and Erik get back with the food.

BO. What?

ROBERT. I dunno. They're not back yet.

BO. Nah.

ROBERT. Nah? Just nah? Did you eat?

BO. I can take care of myself.

ROBERT. Well, good for you. There are some things I brought in the kitchen should you so desire. Things you haven't seen yet. Things you would like. But don't let me tell you what to do.

(BO exits.)

(to himself) Pff...

(BO yells from offstage.)

BO. Why is all the cheese fat free?!

ROBERT. BECAUSE THAT IS HOW WE EAT NOW, you rude little shit.

BO. This isn't food. This is bullshit.

(ROBERT walks off stage, pissed. All off stage:)

What the fuck was your plan man?

ROBERT. What do you mean?

BO. This is so fucked up.

ROBERT. What? *(no answer)* Jesus Christ...it's like –

BO. What? Like never ever having food in the house or getting a fucking neighbor to feed me dinner?

(Sound of snowmobile arriving. The argument intensifies.)

ROBERT. There is food here. And there is more food coming. Listen. That's them! That is them right now!

BO. That's not what I'm talking about! I'm talking about a different thing! New subject!

*(**ROBERT** follows **BO** in to the room.)*

ROBERT. We took you to fabulous restaurants your whole life!

BO. What?!

ROBERT. You know, you / make everything so charged –

BO. You don't even know what it's like to be around you.

ROBERT. The food is here so you can stop / your whining.

BO. You make me want to barf.

*(**HELENE** and **ERIK** enter back in the door from the trading post carrying two big bags.)*

Yo.

*(**BO** exits back to his room.)*

ROBERT. Well, here we go.

HELENE. Yeah, we grabbed what we could. It was kinda a zoo over there. But we got beer, milk, chili mix… I got Equal for those Grapefruits.

ROBERT. Great.

HELENE. Some jar stuff, some fresh stuff and a ton of snacky type stuff. Yadda Yadda you can look.

*(**HELENE** exits toward the kitchen.)*

ROBERT. That's perfect. *(yelling towards the door)* Bo!

BO. FUCK YOU!

ROBERT. Ignore that. Would you two stay for dinner? Please?

ERIK. Oh. Well…we sorta…gotta hike down mountain before it gets too dark.

*(**ERIK** holds up the beer.)*

Hope these aren't frozen.

ROBERT. I will take one of those right now.

ERIK. Careful it doesn't explode.

ROBERT. You tap on the top, you know that trick?

ERIK. Yup.

ROBERT. Join me?

ERIK. Wish I could.

> (**HELENE** *returns, they start getting their backpacks on.*)

HELENE. Alright, let's go.

BO. (*yelling from offstage*) Should I set the table, Papá?

ROBERT. I'm serious. I would really love you guys to stay for dinner. (*quietly*) I can throw you twenty bucks extra.

ERIK. Sorry. Long walk, wolves –

ROBERT. Stay for dinner and then take our snow mobile!

ERIK. I really don't trust it. Starter sounds funky.

ROBERT. I didn't even try the stove. Do you guys know if it's working?

HELENE. Erik checked it out.

ERIK. It's good to go.

> (**ERIK** *opens the sliding door.* **BO** *enters with a box of fruit snacks with a cat cartoon on it.*)

BO. Odie.

ROBERT. What's that?

HELENE. I know it's dorky but they looked kinda good. A lota kids stuff was left 'cause they over-ordered 'cause of the race. Oh! I got you the last bottle of tonic.

ROBERT. Excellent. Let me make you a cocktail.

ERIK. Helene.

ROBERT. Just one cocktail.

BO. My dad always loved drinking with the help.

ERIK. We've got a five mile / hike

ROBERT. Guys...come on. That's crazy. Just stay the night!

> (*They look at each other and consider.*)

HELENE. *(voice over)* So we did.

> *(Lights dim.* **ERIK** *closes they door and they follow* **ROBERT** *across stage and exit. Outside, the sun sets.)*

We can make ourselves very useful. It's something we are good at. The woman who was supposed to work here would never have done as good a job as us.

By the time we finished cleaning up after dinner it was pretty late. Good thing we stayed! Robert brought me something of Jackie's to wear that night, a flannel nightgown from a nice catalog. It smelled like me because I had been wearing it for weeks. *(beat)* We slept well.

Projection: Saturday

(Sunrise through the sliding door. Partially packed boxes of Jackie's things on the floor. Voice over continues.)

HELENE. *(voice over)* The next morning, Robert went out very early to ski the father/son racecourse. He came back to pancakes I made. Bo just slept and slept.

> *(**ROBERT** and **ERIK** enter and set up the NordicTrack facing the sliding door. **ROBERT** hops on and starts NordicTracking. **HELENE** and **ERIK** packing boxes. Voiceover continues.)*

Robert and Bo...but especially Robert...love to talk. A lot.

ROBERT. My ex had all these all these Native American rugs in here and I donated them to Bo's college...his first one. Denison. After he almost got kicked out. The school almost died. They said it was worth a fortune. They were apparently really valuable. I think it was those rugs that held things up in court...with Jackie. That REALLY pissed her off. And cost us both a lot of money. But in the end, 'cause of what I had over her head – Why did we start talking about this?

HELENE. I asked where the basket in the bathroom was from.

ROBERT. Native American. Zuni I think. I think I need to take my morning pills, can you put those together?

> *(**ROBERT** gets off the NordicTrack. **ERIK** folds it up.)*

HELENE. Sure.

ROBERT. You are getting to be my little Nurse and the tall guy is my little handy man...this is working out so well. *(to **ERIK**)* Alright, let's do it.

> *(**HELENE** exits. **ROBERT** and **ERIK** pick up the NordicTrack and carry it towards the door.)*

Helene is so sweet. And she's a real hard worker.

ERIK. Well, she's had to be.

ROBERT. What's that?

ERIK. Just with her upbringing and all.

ROBERT. Did she come from a poor family?

ERIK. She doesn't like talking about it.

ROBERT. I understand. But she *should* talk about it.

>   (*The set the NordicTrack down by the door.*)

ERIK. …Her parents died when she was very young.

ROBERT. Oh no.

ERIK. Very…intense way of going. She saw it all and…oof.

ROBERT. Yeah. (*looks down at the NordicTrack*) I'm sad to see that go. Goodbye old friend.

>   (**ROBERT** *crosses away from* **ERIK.**)

ERIK. So…how were the slopes.

ROBERT. I gotta admit, I'm pretty rusty. Crowded for the big weekend. I tell ya, can't wait to see Bo out there. He's going to be quick in the race. Hope I can keep up.

>   (**ROBERT** *opens the sliding door, pops outside with a "woo!" and grabs a bundle of sticks he's collected.* **ERIK** *watches as* **ROBERT** *walks to the fireplace and starts putting sticks in.*)

Hoping to win the Elk Head award. That's…you know there's the race, but then you stop at these checkpoints and the crowd judges you on different things…and the wacky costume one… I think we can take it. The winner gets a ski boot with a plastic bag in it and you can go in to either of the bars in town and fill it with booze for the whole week. Pretty cool.

ERIK. The fireplace is fake. I mean electric.

ROBERT. Oh. (**ROBERT** *stares at the fireplace, confused.*) Was it always?

ERIK. Um. I guess not. Did you used to burn things in it?

>   (**ROBERT** *thinks.*)

ROBERT. Yeah. Oh. Jackie. Jackie, Jackie, Jackie.

ERIK. Lemme clean those out for ya.

ROBERT. Thank you.

> (ROBERT *watches as* ERIK *pulls the sticks out of the fireplace.* HELENE *enters with pill in hand and a glass of water.* ROBERT *takes the pill. Then he takes her hand and talks to her with gravity and care.*)

Helene. Thank you so very much. I really really appreciate this.

HELENE. Sure.

> (*She glances at* ERIK *who smiles. She exits a little confused.*)

ROBERT. I heard a good one today…let's see…right. How do you know – …What's the difference between a chairlift operator and a pizza?

ERIK. I don't know.

ROBERT. It's supposed to be a large pizza. What's the difference between a chairlift operator and a large pizza?

ERIK. I don't know.

ROBERT. A large pizza can feed a family.

> (ERIK *laughs with* ROBERT.)

ERIK. I like that. In a ski town, you don't get a girlfriend, you get a turn.

> (ROBERT *looks at him. Then:*)

ROBERT. I'm sorry I thought you were making a comment. I didn't realize you were telling a joke. Say again.

> (HELENE *returns.*)

ERIK. In a ski town, you don't get a girlfriend /, you get a turn.

ROBERT. You get a turn. That's a good one.

> (BO *enters as they all laugh*)

BO. Can I borrow a bathing suit?

ROBERT. Good morning.

BO. Can I borrow a bathing suit?

ROBERT. …Yeah.

BO. Mine are like, tiny now.

ROBERT. You take after me downtown.

> (**ROBERT** *winks.* **ERIK** *and* **HELENE** *laugh,* **ROBERT** *enjoys their approval.*)

BO. You are so weird. Forget it.

ROBERT. What?

> (**BO** *exits.* **ERIK** *flips on the switch by fireplace. Orange glowing "embers."*)

Oh! *(Reaches hand out. Leans way in. Disappointed there's no heat.)* Oh.

ERIK. So, you're a writer.

ROBERT. That's right, I *am* an author.

ERIK. What are you writing right now?

ROBERT. Actually, my wife – …ex-wife and I, it's interesting, we started out as just psychologists, but the books sort of caught fire and changed everything. But now we're both moving on to other things. I'm finishing up a brand new one on food and eating right now. Aaaand…she wrote one about divorce. Go figure.

ERIK. *(leaning in, seemingly very interested)* What's the diet?

ROBERT. It's not a diet. It's a mindset, a way of simplifying your food and "the fridge of your mind." That's one of the main concepts.

ERIK. Cool.

ROBERT. Defrosting the fridge of your mind!

ERIK. Wow. Yeah, cool.

> (**HELENE** *and* **ERIK** *are nodding, totally into it.*)

ROBERT. There is a chapter with some recipes though.

ERIK. Oh yeah? Like what?

ROBERT. Well, a lot of veggie broths, steamed stuff, warm lemon water...

ERIK. That's, those are meals?

ROBERT. No that's more of – You want to read it? I have the galleys...

ERIK. Yeah, I'd love to check it out.

HELENE. Yeah, me too.

ROBERT. Great.

> (**ERIK** *switches off the fireplace.*)

ERIK. I'm going to give the satellite another go. I'll get this working for you, Robert.

> (**ERIK** *turns on the TV. Silent static. He turns to look at* **ROBERT**.)

(earnestly) I cooked a lot with my dad growing up. I wanna get back into that. It would be fun to try some of those recipes.

ROBERT. *(touched)* Great. Love it. Erik, don't kill yourself over the TV. We can call the guys down at whatever that place is called now.

ERIK. They're closed.

> (**ERIK** *exits.*)

HELENE. Erik's dad passed away a couple months ago, I'm so sorry if he is being a little weird.

ROBERT. Oh my God. No, not at all. He's such a sweetie.

HELENE. *(earnestly)* He's an only child, so...it's just him now. It's a lot. He doesn't like to talk about it, so... ANYway. This whole box of stuff is not on the list. Should it go in the donation pile?

ROBERT. Just give them to Jackie.

> (**BO** *enters in super tight swimming trunks. He climbs in the Jacuzzi.*)

Gonna take a little dip?

BO. ...Yep. (*quietly to himself*) What does it look like?

HELENE. Oh, Robert. I found those bandanas you were looking for.

ROBERT. Oh great! Can I see?

> (HELENE *gets up and walks to the bag by* ROBERT.)

Helene found the matching bandanas.

BO. Cool.

ROBERT. Remember we used to tie them on our right feet in the boot buckles.

BO. What?

ROBERT. For our costumes. For the race. Right fight! Right fight! In the snow! We win tonight!

BO. I don't remember that at all.

ROBERT. Helene, they do a greased pig chase where ya chase a pig on skies.

BO. It's really funny.

ROBERT. Very fun.

BO. It's a huge mess. Someone always breaks a leg.

ROBERT. Been doing it since the '30s, commemorative for...something. Goes to a good cause.

BO. No it doesn't.

ROBERT. *(to* HELENE*)* Rocky Mountain Rendezvous is what the fur trappers called their annual gathering to sell their furs. Before trading posts, they would get together / once a year and trade and celebrate.

BO. I'm sure she knows that, Dad, everybody here knows that.

ROBERT. I'm just telling her that the weekend / has a context and a history –

BO. She lives here. She lives here. She knows this.

ROBERT. Alright. Alright. Sorry.

> (ROBERT *rolls his eyes towards* HELENE. HELENE *laughs.* BO *takes it all in.* ROBERT *exits.)*

BO. Helene.

HELENE. Yeah?

BO. Do you know anything about ski wax?

HELENE. Do you need me to wax your skis?

BO. OK.

> (*He turns away and turns on the Jacuzzi jets.*)

HELENE. Which skis are yours?

BO. Yellow Atombombs.

HELENE. I can do that later.

> (*beat*)

Erik and I read your dad's book.

BO. Does it suck?

HELENE. No, it's really interesting.

BO. Did you lose weight?

HELENE. No, we read the one about you.

> (**BO** *looks at* **HELENE**. **ROBERT** *enters with a towel around his waist, he opens the towel to get in.*)

BO. Dad. No. You gotta wear something in here.

ROBERT. (*to himself*) Jeez.

> (**ROBERT** *exits, disappointed.*)

BO. Can you turn the temp up?

HELENE. It's right on the side.

BO. I know.

> (**HELENE** *turns up the temp.* **BO** *closes his eyes.* **HELENE** *watches him for a beat too long.*)

HELENE. Where are you going next?

BO. Probably Switzerland for a buddy's wedding. Or I might have to sail this dumb regatta.

HELENE. Really?

BO. Yeah.

HELENE. I thought you had to go back to some girl in Romania or something? I don't know why I thought that.

(**ROBERT** *returns in bathing suit.*)

BO. Why did you say that?

HELENE. Say what?

(**ROBERT** *starts climbing in the Jacuzzi.*)

ROBERT. Incoming ship. (**BO** *doesn't move.*) I'm serious Bo, scooch over.

(**ROBERT** *gets comfortable.* **BO** *turns off the jets.* **ROBERT** *looks at* **BO**, *smiles and nods.*)

Not bad, right? I always said this place needed a Jacuzzi.

BO. Yup.

ROBERT. It's so relaxing. Right Bo? Mm?

(**ROBERT** *starts doing a ridiculous stretch.*)

I'm doing a lot of physical therapy and stretches. I was gonna fly Sarah my trainer out but that would be weird for Bo. We were intimate when my back went out for the first time. That would be weird for Bo. If she was here now. We were sleeping together when I was still with Jackie. But by then we were both sleeping with every – What was my point?

HELENE. I don't know.

ROBERT. I don't know. Her body's dynamite. Mm.

HELENE. You guys gonna win that race?

BO. (*quietly*) Nope.

ROBERT. No way. It's not really about the race though… It's more the event of it.

BO. Dad. They read Making Bobby Robert.

HELENE. It's great.

BO. It's great in Junior High to have everyone know about your first boner.

ROBERT. Well your first erections are when you're a baby. You're talking about –

BO. She knows what I'm talking about. She read the book. (*getting upset*) Did you give it to them? Are there copies here? You promised –

ROBERT. Bo. Bo. Calm down. I dunno.

(**ERIK** *pops in the sliding door.*)

ERIK. Anything?

(**HELENE** *looks at the TV screen.*)

HELENE. Nope.

ERIK. I'm gonna need another day to figure this out.

BO. Hey is that mine? Was that mine?

ERIK. What?

BO. That coat.

ERIK. I don't know. Is it?

BO. …it's cool.

ERIK. It was in a bag your dad wants to donate.

BO. To like poor people?

ROBERT. Whoa. Bo.

ERIK. You can have it back man.

BO. No No NO. (**BO** *gets out of the tub and crosses to the door.*) Hey, I'm not gonna wear a costume Dad.

ROBERT. Yeah, right.

BO. I'm serious.

(**ERIK** *pulls the section of co-ax cable out of his pocket and attaches it to the TV.*)

ROBERT. I ordered them from California and you are joking right?

BO. No.

ROBERT. Everyone loves the costumes.

BO. Kids and really old people. I'm not wearing a costume.

(*He exits. The TV flickers on.*)

ERIK. Boom!

HELENE. Nice!

ERIK. TV's fixed.

(*They look at* **ROBERT** *who is looking at the door where* **BO** *exited. Blackout.*)

Saturday Afternoon

(**ROBERT** *folds towels.* **HELENE** *walks in.*)

ROBERT. Fold with me, Helene!

HELENE. Which way do you do your towels?

ROBERT. Doesn't matter.

> (*They fold.* **ERIK** *enters with a box, nudges her as he puts it next to her.*)

This has been nice.

HELENE. It has been nice, Robert. (*holding up a patterned towel*) I love this one.

ROBERT. (*sad to see it go*) Yeeeah…

HELENE. Why does she want all the towels?

ROBERT. Exactly.

> (**ERIK** *pulls things down off the wall.* **HELENE** *and* **ROBERT** *quietly fold. They smile at each other.*)

HELENE. Where's Bo?

ROBERT. Probably disappeared. He just shows up whenever and leaves whenever. That's atypical second child behavior but it's, you know. That's how he does it. He once left me in Disney World after getting pissed at me for something. That was a New Year's I'll never forget.

HELENE. Yeah. I hate that holiday.

> (**ROBERT** *does a loooong exhale.*)

Yep.

ROBERT. We shoulda stopped while we were ahead. Jackie wanted a girl or to try for one. And there was all this only child fear, everyone was kinda –

> (*Phone rings.* **HELENE** *and* **ERIK** *both make a move for it.*)

Leave it for the machine.

> (*As the phone rings,* **HELENE** *and* **ERIK** *glance at each other.* **ERIK** *makes his way to the door and*

closes it. Behind it, on the wall for decoration, hang old rusty tools. **ERIK** *pulls down the wrench.)*

ROBERT. *(cont.)* Parenting's weird, man. The irony of that, coming from me, that's, you know. I get it. I tell ya, it would have been so easy with one. Well, then I wouldn't have done the books.

ANSWERING MACHINE. *(HELENE's voice)* Hi we're not here right now. At the message leave us a beep. BEEEP. *(MAN's voice)* Hi, Centennial Vacation Home Services. / Sorry to call again, we're still trying to sort all this out about Helene Douglass. If –

(HELENE makes a move for the phone. ROBERT waves her off.)

ROBERT. I got it. *(picks up the phone)* Hello, Robert Elder... Sure... I'm sorry, let me stop you, she's right here... Helene... Yeah. Right here. And Erik too... Erik... The tall guy *(away from the phone)* What's your last name again? *(ERIK, wrench at his side, stares blankly. Back on the phone:)* Say again... Uh, I'm sorry, I'm not sure – ... When? When did I talk to you? ...Uhhh, no.

(HELENE takes the phone out of his hands.)

HELENE. *(into the phone)* Don't ever call back here again!

(She slams down the phone. ROBERT stares.)

ROBERT. What's going on guys?

(HELENE and ERIK, on either side of ROBERT, look at each other for a long time. ROBERT looks at ERIK then back at HELENE. ERIK, gripping wrench tightly, takes a step toward ROBERT. HELENE suddenly starts crying and covers her face. She walks away from ROBERT, licking her fingers and wiping her face to make "tears." She crumples into a chair, ROBERT rushes to her side.)

HELENE. Erik...you tell him.

ERIK. Me?

HELENE. Yeah.

(**ROBERT** *stares at him.*)

ERIK. OK. Oh boy. *(He exhales. Long pause.)* A manager at Centennial... Doug...was really inappropriate with Helene. He was kinda in love with her and it got pretty messed up. He kept trying to kiss her...smell her hair. He'd say things. He got fired because of it and now he calls every place we work, making stuff up, trying to mess with us.

ROBERT. This guy's name was Joe.

(*Beat.* **ERIK** *unsure what to say.*)

HELENE. *(sobbing)* That's what he said this time?

ROBERT. Oh.

HELENE. I'm sorry Robert. This is embarrassing.

ROBERT. What a jerk!

HELENE. Yeah. I'm ok. I'm sorry. Can we just forget about it?

ROBERT. Do you want me to –

HELENE. No! Let's just forget about it.

(**ROBERT** *looks to* **ERIK**, *who nods.*)

ROBERT. Sure.

(**ROBERT** *rubs her shoulder.* **HELENE** *smiles, laughs, "shakes it out."* **BO** *enters from outside in ski boots.*)

BO. What I miss? You all like bonding and shit?

ROBERT. ...How were the trails?

BO. Super crowded. Lot of people dressed like dumb things.

ROBERT. *(excited)* Oh yeah! Like what?

BO. You know...the banana sombero guy, the old lady with the bikini over her ski suit. It's all the same just everyone is like really old.

HELENE. There's lunch for you on the counter.

BO. Sweet.

(**BO** *crosses to the other door, clomping awkwardly in ski boots. Everyone watches. He exits.*)

HELENE. Um… Erik!

(*She pulls out two papier mâché masks. She puts one of them on.*)

ERIK. Yeah? Oh. Wow.

HELENE. Cool.

ROBERT. Pretty cool, right?

HELENE. Yeah.

ERIK. Those are great.

(*She slides the mask up to the top of her head.*)

ROBERT. Good times. We did a lot of mask work over the years. Powerful stuff.

(**ERIK** *exits.*)

Jackie won't want that fur coat now that she's a Buddhist. I spent our first advance on it 'cause she had to have it. Helene, would you like it?

HELENE. No thanks.

ROBERT. As a bonus for all the work you've been doing?

HELENE. No thanks, furs kinda scare me.

ROBERT. Really?

HELENE. Yeah, they kinda creep me out…but thanks.

(*She puts the masks back in the box.* **BO** *comes in eating soup, does another awkward ski boot cross.*)

BO. Soup.

HELENE. Yep.

(**BO** *turns on the TV and flips through channels.* **ERIK** *returns with a smallish box and hands it to* **HELENE.** *They share a look.* **ERIK** *exits.*)

Here's a box we put together. It's things we're not sure what to do with. Bo stuff mostly. Can you guys take a look and figure it out?

ROBERT. Oh sure. (**ROBERT** *digs through the box.*) Mmm, these are Bo's little cowboy boots. And moccasins! Hey Bo take a look at these. Hey, you used to put your teeth in this for the tooth fairy.

(**BO** *turns off the TV.*)

BO. I'm going to ski down to town.

ROBERT. You were just out.

BO. Yep.

ROBERT. Just sit down for a sec – Did you just roll your eyes?

BO. Probably.

ROBERT. Robert Michael if you –

BO. How old am I how old am I how old am I?!

ROBERT. Bobby!

(**HELENE** *quickly exits.*)

BO. You probably don't even know how fucking old I am!

ROBERT. How old am I?!

BO. You drag me out here, you / have no idea –

ROBERT. HERE we go. Blame me. Blame me. I really just wanted this to be a nice weekend.

BO. I'm not talking. I'm out of here.

ROBERT. Robert Michael –

BO. Oh my God oh my God oh my GOD! What was I just saying! I have NO –

(*Suddenly, a screaming fight in the kitchen. It briefly overlaps with and then stops* **ROBERT** *and* **BO**'s *fight.*)

ERIK. Just give it to me!

HELENE. What?!

ERIK. Here!

HELENE. Don't put that in there!

ERIK. You just told me to!

HELENE. What?

ERIK. You told me *today* that –

HELENE. That's not what I'm talking about!

ERIK. What? *(No answer)* Jesus Christ…it's like –

HELENE. What?

ERIK. Let me finish let me finish!

HELENE. LOOK AT ME!

ERIK. I AM looking at you!

HELENE. DON'T LOOK AT ME!

> *(ROBERT and BO stare at each other. HELENE and ERIK return with boxes, sit and calmly resume looking through things. ROBERT and BO watch them as they work and then start rummaging through the box together.)*

ERIK. *(holding up a T-shirt)* Helene, these are cool, right?

> *(Front of T-shirt says "Today's Boy." He turns it, back reads "Tomorrow's Man.")*

HELENE. Mm-hm. *(holding up a sweater)* This is pretty.

ROBERT. That was Jackie's.

HELENE. It's nice.

> *(She puts it on.)*

BO. Those T-shirts are from when Mom and Dad were famous.

ROBERT. Well, I don't know if I'd say *famous*.

BO. It felt like you were famous.

ROBERT. Well…yeah. We were pretty well known. The first book was big in child development circles. Or maybe I should say *controversial* and that's always good. But then the follow ups, boy, those – that's what really…which that was the intention: more mainstream, less –

BO. They had tapes and T-shirts.

> *(ERIK and HELENE hold up cassette tapes. Like the books, young BO is on the cover.)*

ROBERT. That's right, we did.

BO. When my parents were on Donahue they locked me in the hotel room and told me not to watch TV and –

ROBERT. Bo –

BO. You did! You / know you did that! You –

ROBERT. Bobobo, I know. I'm saying I know. *(beat)* Toss those. Get rid of it. Throw it away. Throw all of that away.

> *(**ERIK** exits with the box.)*

So let's see…

> *(**ROBERT** pulls out a tape.)*

Oh my god.

> *(**ROBERT** makes his way to the tape player. **BO** picks up the tiny boots.)*

BO. Can I keep these?

ROBERT. Ahhhh. No. I wish you could.

BO. Aren't they mine?

ROBERT. There's a list. Your mother has a list. It all needs to go back to her.

BO. Can I ask her for them?

ROBERT. That's, you know, that's up to you. Yes. Yes, you should ask her for them.

BO. I will.

> *(**ROBERT** puts the tape on. It's a recording of a kid playing a classical song on recorder. **ERIK** returns.)*

HELENE. What this?

ROBERT. Bo at eleven. He was good.

> *(They all listen. **HELENE** quietly exits. **ERIK** turns on the fireplace and exits. After a moment **ROBERT** exits. **BO** is alone. The tape plays to the end.)*

Saturday Night

*(Nighttime. The lights in the Jacuzzi and fireplace
are on, and nothing else.* **HELENE** *smokes a joint
outside.)*

HELENE. *(voice over)* A month ago I called Sean. He was
excited to hear from me again. He had grown out
his beard and was seeing some girl ten years younger
than him. She thought his name was Troy. Which I still
think is funny. He got here as soon as he could. And
then Helene from Centennial Home Services showed
up. We enjoyed that. I smashed my arm with a wrench
when she picked up the phone to report us. Poor
thing. She was screaming more than I was.

> *(***ROBERT*** *enters the living room in a swimsuit and
> bathrobe. He turns on the Jacuzzi bubbles, notices
> ***HELENE*** *outside and opens the sliding door.)*

ROBERT. Where did you get the doobie?

HELENE. It's mine.

ROBERT. Can I join you?

HELENE. Sure.

> *(***ROBERT*** *goes outside with* ***HELENE*** *and they
> smoke, hopping around in the freezing cold and
> laughing. They open the door and rush back
> inside.* ***ROBERT*** *takes off his robe and jumps in
> the Jacuzzi.* ***HELENE*** *takes off her jacket and
> pants, revealing a man's undershirt and boxers.
> She puts her plastic bag over her cast and gets in
> the Jacuzzi.)*

ROBERT. Bubbles off maybe?

HELENE. Yeah.

ROBERT. Is it alright if I turn the light off?

HELENE. Sure.

ROBERT. You can see outside better with it off.

(He turns off the Jacuzzi light. Darkness except for the night sky through the glass door and the fireplace.)

ROBERT. Colorado.

HELENE. Yeah. We visited Erik's uncle in Argentina. His ranch. Very pretty, but not like this. He *did* have wild Clydesdales though.

ROBERT. Jackie absolutely would have me killed if she could have me killed.

HELENE. That's how it goes. Fuck you Jackie!

(They laugh.)

Hey Robert... Bo was telling me, and... I guess he wouldn't want me to say anything, but... I think it's important.

ROBERT. ...OK.

HELENE. No, it just... He said that he's glad he came here. And that it's hard for him to talk about, but, he was really concerned about your... *(She gestures around his heart.)*

ROBERT. What?

HELENE. Health stuff.

ROBERT. Health stuff? *(a beat of confusion)* My polyps?

HELENE. Yeah. That was really scary for him.

ROBERT. Wow. I didn't know he knew about that.

HELENE. Yeah.

ROBERT. No, there's no way he could of known that. Who did I tell? *(long beat)* Oh!

HELENE. Yeah, I think that's why he didn't say anything. I think he was a little shaken by how hard he took it.

ROBERT. Wow. I dunno. Wasn't a very big deal.

HELENE. Yeaaaah.

ROBERT. Thank you, Helene.

HELENE. Hey.

(He smiles at her for a while.)

ROBERT. What do you do for fun?

HELENE. For fun?

ROBERT. Yeah. What do you like to do?

HELENE. Good question…um…

ROBERT. It's a stumper!

HELENE. I guess…just…doing stuff like this.

ROBERT. Me too.

> (**BO** *comes in. Turns on the light.*)

BO. Oh god!

> (*Turns light back off, turns to go.*)

ROBERT. No, no, come on in. Join us.

BO. That's cool.

ROBERT. No, no. We have a spot for you right here.

BO. You sure?

HELENE. Yeah.

> (**BO** *turns on the light. They wave at him. He turns off the light. He crosses to the tub.*)

ROBERT. Good skiing?

BO. Yeah.

> (**BO** *gets in.*)

ROBERT. You know, I was thinking…maybe no race tomorrow. I just don't know if I'm in the mood for that. What do you think Bo? Up to you. You'll get the money either way. You call it. Want to think about it?

BO. Yeah. I'll think about it.

HELENE. I don't know. Sounds like a lot of fun to me.

ROBERT. Well, let's have fun tonight, huh Helene?

HELENE. *(very direct)* Get us some wine.

> (**ROBERT** *laughs.*)

ROBERT. You got it!

> (**ROBERT** *gets out of the Jacuzzi and exits.* **HELENE** *stares at* **BO** *for a while. He turns away from her.*)

HELENE. Your dad was just saying he's glad you came here.

BO. Pft.

HELENE. Sorry. I'll change the subject. *(She nonchalantly floats closer to him.)* Poor guy. It's been a rough time for your dad.

BO. This divorce stuff has been –

HELENE. No, I mean with the cancer scare and everything and I think because he's –

BO. What wait what?

HELENE. Oh. Oops. He probably didn't want to scare you. You know what… I'm sure it helps just having you here with him.

> *(**ROBERT** returns with a bottle of wine and three mismatched mugs.)*

ROBERT. Never told you where your mother hid the good stuff. Just one glass, right Bo?

BO. This is trippy.

ROBERT. What's trippy?

BO. Being here.

ROBERT. Well…yeah.

BO. Dad pretty much blackmailed Mom to get this place.

ROBERT. It wasn't blackmail. *(He pours the wine into the mugs and passes them out.)* It was…using information…to negotiate a fair settlement.

BO. OK.

ROBERT. It was!

HELENE. Cheers!

ROBERT. Helene.

HELENE. Yeah?

> *(**ERIK** enters in the dark, in his underwear. He slowly crosses towards the tub.)*

ROBERT. I like the old names. I had a great aunt *Helen.*

HELENE. Oh yeah?

ROBERT. Diabetic very large woman. Very sweet. Hm. I wonder if that got me into nutrition? You never think about those things until so late! Hm. I'm grateful. Here's to you. *(He raises his mug to the sky. Then towards* **HELENE**.*)* Helene, to your parents too. *(He notices* **ERIK**.*)* And to Erik's dad. Grab yourself a glass, Erik.

ERIK. We can share.

> *(He takes* **BO**'s *cup out of his hand.* **ROBERT** *raises his glass to the sky.)*

ROBERT. "May you be in heaven a full half hour before the devil knows you're dead."

> *(They all drink.* **ERIK** *drinks from* **BO**'s *glass.* **BO** *eyes him.)*

It's been a tough year for him. He was traveling a lot. I did the same thing. I was like what am I gonna learn here when I can see the world. Of course, I saved up to do that. That's the other thing. I grew up without any money. Philadelphia. And not the Main Line. *Philly* Philly. So it meant something different to me. Bo I think *tried* to find himself but didn't really get the rhythm of it all. I fell in love a million times and Bo kind of obsesses on one girl for years. I think he must have still been sad from…Jeany –

BO. Jenny.

ROBERTS. – breaking his heart. Drank too much. Which we have that problem in our family. My ex-wife is a raging alcoholic.

BO. That's not exactly what happened. I got cut off because my parents were trying to show some authority.

ROBERT. You stood your mother up in Paris.

BO. That's not what happened. She –

ROBERT. I don't want to get back into it.

BO. Soooo for money a buddy of mine knew a guy who was looking for waiters. I never fucking waited tables /

ROBERT. I waited tables all through / college.

(**ERIK** *sits on the edge.*)

BO. didn't know shit about that. And actually it ended up being more like busboys because I speak French so bad. (**HELENE** *and* **ERIK** *look at each other, then start laughing at* **BO***'s story.* **BO** *gets more and more into it*) So I'm suddenly like all dressed in black and white in this crazy five star restaurant. And I don't know shit about how to set stuff down or forks…like I never thought about that crap. I just ate /

ROBERT. Forks on the left, right side you –

BO. And then one night I got roped into taking care of this guy's girlfriend from the restaurant and I ended up getting sliced by a broken candle thing when a fight broke out cuz she was like actually married to some prince or sheik or whatever. That's what this thing is on my hand.

ROBERT. Where?

BO. You should see this thing on my ass.

ROBERT. What?

BO. This was this other time. It actually was pretty funny. I was at a party and I convinced the host I could do magic. I had some drinks and I got up on this table 'cause it was like my stage…and the *whole* party was watching, like over two hundred people probably and I was making up magic tricks with cards, but they were like totally fake.

(**HELENE** *and* **ERIK** *are loving it,* **BO** *is holding court and* **ROBERT** *is starting to enjoy it too.*)

People were into it for a while because they couldn't understand what I was saying. I was trying to impress this woman I sorta fell for and – um.

(**BO** *stops dead in his tracks*)

Ah. Forget about it. Just some dumb lady I fell for. *(changing the subject)* Hey, remember all the parties *here?*

ROBERT. Oh God yes! Jackie and I used to have little parties for the kids on the mountain, where we'd have them over and feed them, they'd watch a movie and then we'd use the kids to develop the exercises for the book, you know try – test out some of our theories and –

BO. That's what those parties were for?

ROBERT. Of course.

BO. Oh man, of course. *(laughs a little)*

ROBERT. We talked about it back then. You knew.

BO. Maybe.

ROBERT. When we put all the kid's names in the special thanks.

BO. Yeah, I guess I remember that.

ROBERT. Anyway, that's not the point. There was one party where –

BO. Graham Kudler!

ROBERT. Right!

BO. Dad. Graham Kudler. Yes. I totally forgot. Oh my God.

ROBERT. Graham Kudler was –

BO. This kid who came from a really crazy family. Like they could only wear certain colors and his parents wouldn't let him like eat / anything that –

ROBERT. Wait, what with the color?

BO. They weren't allowed, he and his brothers or sisters, weren't allowed to wear certain colors because of the chemicals in the dye or something.

ROBERT. Wow. *That* I did not know.

BO. This kid was really good looking.

ROBERT. His parents were models. Or his mom was. And his dad was something cool.

BO. So they lived in California and had weird clothes and would come to Colorado for vacation. He was here for my birthday party –

ROBERT. One of these parties where Jackie and I were testing interactions between –

BO. Yeah and he shows up – …Wait. Dad. My *birthday* party was one of those parties?

ROBERT. Yep.

BO. Oh my God. That is so fucked up.

ROBERT. Why?

BO. Anyway, so we're playing this game – …let me back up. We're all making masks out of homemade papier mâché. Have you done that before?

HELENE. Yeah.

ERIK. No

ROBERT. They've seen the masks.

BO. What?!

ROBERT. I found the masks. That's why I'm telling you.

BO. No way! Erik: alright, so you dip strips of newspaper into this stuff and put it on your face.

ERIK. Mm-hm.

ROBERT. But you have to put Vaseline on or it will stick.

ERIK. OK.

(**BO** *and* **ROBERT** *are really getting into it.*)

ROBERT. All the kids have their masks on and they wait for them to dry and they're going to take them off to paint them but Graham's was stuck. Because he didn't use Vaseline like he was supposed to.

BO. And he just started freaking out and ripping it off his face, and it was all dried and his eyebrows were stuck to it.

ERIK. Oh my god!

BO. Yeah and he was like running around bleeding, freaking all the kids out…it looked like patches were cheese gratered or something where he tore it off.

ROBERT. Well, that's not quite right. Jackie did have to cut a little bit of his hair off, but he was able to soak in the tub with some Epsom salts and the mask came right off.

BO. Well then why did he run out into the snow?

ROBERT. I think the Epsom salt burned his eyes or something

BO. I just remember him bleeding and running in the snow headfirst.

ROBERT. Nope.

> *(beat)*

BO. Well, his parents freaked and never let him come over again.

ROBERT. Yeah.

> *(beat)*

Well... Great house for entertaining.

> *(Transition:* **BO** *drinks,* **ROBERT** *gets out of the Jacuzzi and goes outside,* **ERIK** *gets in the tub.* **ROBERT** *is outside peeing.)*

Wooooo!

HELENE. He does mural painting here in the summer at the day camp.

BO. Camp Turtle Lake?!

ERIK. Yep.

BO. I went there! Do they still –

ERIK. Neat. She works for someone in the summers that – I guess you're not supposed to say –

HELENE. Yeah, I'm not really allowed to say.

> *(***HELENE** *and* **ERIK** *laugh.)*

BO. That's funny. Cheers! Hey, remind me Helene, are your parents still married or are they dead? ...How about yours... Derek?

> *(beat)*

Let me ask you this, what were you gonna do with all our stuff?

> *(He smiles. Nailed 'em.* **ROBERT** *has returned and is getting in the tub. He's drunk.* **HELENE** *and*

ERIK *look at each other.* ERIK *smiles and nods at* BO.)

ROBERT. Now the history of this house is pretty interesting, this was Ute land, U-T-E until a massacre and such and they got kicked over into Utah. That's not really about this house, just the history of the area that was backback. And when the silver mines and the railroad came through that's about the point when Jackie's Uncle came out here, that would be 1936, and he – Well I'll back up. *(He makes a rewind noise.)* That was New Deal times and this was a comfort station put up by the forestry department but Jackie's Uncle, he passed in World War II, he had some kind of a thing with somebody over in Washington and he fell in love with this plot and bought it and then Jackie's dad brought in his own guy to redo it. Do you know the skiing around here came about after the war when soldiers who had done alpine training here came back and started up the industry. And Jackie's family was already by then pretty established so they got in on that too.

(ROBERT *takes a drink.*)

HELENE. We should get a picture.

ERIK. I'll get your camera.

(ERIK *grabs a towel and exits. After a moment,* HELENE *starts to get out of the Jacuzzi.*)

ROBERT. Erik's such a nice guy.

HELENE. Yeah. He's just really smart and has a lot of opinions about stuff. I like that. *(yelling)* Erik! Erik!!

(HELENE *runs after* ERIK.)

ROBERT. Uh-oh. What's that about?

(They sit quietly in the water.)

I'm all pruny. We should get out soon, right?

BO. Dad, when is all the stuff getting picked up?

ROBERT. Monday morning. Then I have a flight.

BO. Maybe I'll stick around and help you.

*(A moment. **ROBERT** puts his hand on **BO**'s shoulder.)*

ROBERT. Great.

BO. Are you excited? About the book?

ROBERT. Yes. Yes I am. I'm little nervous. People seem to like it.

BO. Cassie still your agent?

*(**ERIK** and **HELENE** stand in the dark doorway, wearing the papier-mâché masks.)*

ROBERT. Yeah, she is.

BO. Cool. She was always nice.

ROBERT. Nice lady.

*(**ERIK** and **HELENE** slowly walk toward the Jacuzzi. **BO** and **ROBERT** watch in silence, then:)*

Graham, what are you doing here? You got so tall!

*(**ERIK** and **HELENE** laugh. **ERIK** pretends to try to pull his mask off.)*

ERIK. Ahhh, it's stuck!

*(They all laugh again, **BO** a little uneasily. **HELENE** sets up the camera on the edge of the Jacuzzi.)*

HELENE. Alright guys, smush together.

*(They smush. She sets the timer and joins **ERIK** standing behind the guys. **BO** grimaces. **ROBERT** makes a funny face. **HELENE** and **ERIK**, wearing the masks, stare blankly.)*

ERIK. Ahhh!

(Everyone laughs.)

ROBERT. You guys.

(They camera flashes. They take that masks off.)

Time for a treat. How's the VCR?

ERIK & HELENE. How's the VCR?

ROBERT. It works?

ERIK. Oh yeah.

ROBERT. Beautiful.

> (**ROBERT** *rummages through a shoebox by the TV and pulls out a video cassette.*)

Movie time! Hey! *(points at* **HELENE***)* Helene, do you have any more of that grass on you?

HELENE. No, I just had that one joint.

BO. What's this, Dad?

ROBERT. Jackie had these transferred.

BO. Oh no. Dad.

ROBERT. Shshsh. Yer not in these. Take a chill pill.

> (*He puts a tape in the VCR. They watch. Old family 8mm movies.*)

> (*young man in a boat*)

That's your uncle Clark. The brother.

> (*older man in a boat*)

Jackie's mom's dad, your great grandpa.

> (*Jackie comes on the screen, splashing in water.* **BO** *moves to the middle of the Jacuzzi. Rapt.*)

BO. Oh my God. *(beat)* How old is she?

ROBERT. Sixteen, Seventeen? Fifteen?

BO. You didn't know her then.

ROBERT. Yeah, this is a couple years before we met. This is in the lake here.

> (*Video switches to Bullfighting.* **ERIK** *and* **HELENE** *watch them watch.*)

Whoa.

BO. Where is this where is this what is this?

ROBERT. I honestly don't remember where this…this is Seville probably. Maybe. I went to a few of these. When I was, uh, after college.

HELENE. Wow.

BO. Do they just kill it like that?

ROBERT. No, no. At the end they take a sword – ...what's the sword called...

HELENE. *(quietly)* Estoque.

ROBERT. ...I don't remember. It goes between the shoulder blades and zhoop, into the heart. I missed that part though, I was reloading the camera so –. *There*, see you can see now the sword is in now and watch. See... whoop. There he goes.

> (**ERIK** *and* **HELENE** *exit. The movies continue; other family events.*)

BO. ...I ran into my buddy Brant today. He says hi. He's letting us borrow something to wear for tomorrow.

ROBERT. What is it?

BO. It's like...an accessory. I'll pick it up in the morning and meet you at the starting line. It's good. I don't want to give it away.

ROBERT. ...Cool.

BO. *(almost breaking)* I'm a little buzzed.

ROBERT. Me too. That's ok.

BO. Dad.

ROBERT. Yes, Bo?

BO. *(breaking)* Oh my God. Dad.

ROBERT. What can I do, Bo?

BO. I have to tell you something.

ROBERT. OK.

BO. I did something bad.

ROBERT. OK.

BO. It's not going to be ok. *(beat)* I really messed up.

> (**ROBERT**, *still wearing his robe, climbs into the tub and hugs* **BO**. *Lights fade.*)

HELENE. *(voice over)* Ah. Colorado. I'm sad we have to go. I've heard it's nice in the spring. But it's changing here. The snowboarders are coming. Taking over the slopes.

THAT will really change things. Soon I bet there will be even more resorts on this land where there used to be silver mines and before that there were tuberculosis sanatoriums and before that Ute Villages. Maybe someday this house will be torn down to make way for condos or a new chairlift or something. That's sad to think about. Maybe that's when they'll find the charred bones of a long missing woman in the bottom of the old trash barrel. But that's a long time from now.

In a few days, Jackie will receive the boxes of her smashed collectables. We're bad at packing. We're good at breaking things. Satellites, bones, snowmobiles. But right now...it's Rocky Mountain Rendezvous. Father/ son race day. And the conditions are perfect. Sunny and cold with that dusting of powder that makes you feel like you're floating.

> *(Lit only by the Jacuzzi light,* **HELENE** *and* **ERIK** *slowly cover the tub.)*

Projection: Sunday

> *(Lights bump up,* **HELENE** *and* **ERIK** *stand with their hands on covered Jacuzzi.* **ERIK** *crosses and takes off his wig. Sound of a gun shot in the distance.)*

ERIK. Shit. Race just started.

HELENE. Do a walk through.

> *(***ERIK*** *leaves his wig on the sideboard and quickly exits.* **HELENE** *quickly puts on her boots and puts a note on the Jacuzzi cover.* **ROBERT** *suddenly enters from the sliding door in an elaborate, over the top ski costume. Perhaps a pharaoh.)*

Hi!

ROBERT. Is Bo here?

HELENE. No.

ROBERT. He didn't show.

HELENE. What?

ROBERT. Bo didn't show.

> *(***ROBERT*** *turns away for a moment, removing some of his costume headgear.* **HELENE** *discretely grabs the note off the tub.)*

HELENE. Erik! Wait...what?

ROBERT. Yeah. I don't know. I don't know what to do.

HELENE. ...Are you ok?

> *(***ERIK*** *enters and unseen by* **ROBERT** *calmly puts his wig on.* **ROBERT** *is agitated.)*

ROBERT. Yeah. Yeah. No, it's just we had a talk last night, and Bo had things he was scared to tell me about, pretty serious stuff... I, ya know, I had no idea... Hi Erik. Bo didn't show.

ERIK. What?

ROBERT. We had a big, big talk last night. And he – I think he's... Oh boy. The race was too too much for me to expect of him. Emotionally. How do I look!? Pretty goofy, right?

ERIK. Yeah. It's good.

HELENE. You look great.

ROBERT. I led him through some therapies, some exercises you know, just... I don't know what else to do. There's not really... I'm sorry guys I just need to respect Bo's privacy. I know you care about him too. He did some things, whatever comes of it – He never feels bad about stuff, at least not that I ever saw, but he really felt bad, which...

HELENE. *(soothing)* Which is good.

ROBERT. Which is good.

> (**ROBERT** *sits on the edge of the Jacuzzi cover.* **HELENE** *and* **ERIK** *stare at it.*)

If there's a trial or or or or – ... *(choking back tears)* whatever comes of it. Whatever comes of it. I'm going to be there with him.

ERIK. It's hard stuff.

ROBERT. Yep. Oh boy. Well...what can you do.

> (*They stand there quietly.*)

ERIK. Everything's in good shape here. The path is cleared –

HELENE. The boxes are ready to go and they'll be picked up tomorrow.

> (**ROBERT** *gets up and crosses away.* **HELENE** *follows him.* **ERIK** *stands by the Jacuzzi.*)

ROBERT. Great. Can you guys stick around for the BBQ?

HELENE. No, we gotta get down mountain before everyone else does. Miss the crowds.

ROBERT. Well, good. I've kept you here. I tell you what... drop by sometime, maybe we can all –

HELENE. I thought you were heading out?

ROBERT. I'm gonna stick around for a bit. You know just... I dunno. Just in case.

HELENE. We um…we're leaving.

ROBERT. Like leaving leaving?

HELENE. Yeah! We've been thinking about it for a while. Getting out. You sort of encouraged us, I guess.

ROBERT. *(pointing to the note in* **HELENE***'s hand)* What's that?

HELENE. You caught us. We were writing you guys a note. We're bad at goodbyes.

> *(***ROBERT*** holds out his hand. Beat.* **HELENE** *hands it to him.* **ROBERT** *reads the note. He looks up at them.)*

ROBERT. Me too you guys. Is this the four of us?

HELENE. Yeah, it's just a doodle. You're the bear.

ERIK. Big Bear Boozer!

ROBERT. Well…this is sad. Man. Here. *(***ROBERT*** writes on a piece of paper.)* This is my address in Philly. You guys have to come visit me there. You guys will get such a kick out of it. Real hip city. Lot of history. That's where I grew up.

HELENE. *(looking down at the address)* We will.

ERIK. Well…we'll see ya next time, Robert.

ROBERT. Aww, love you guys. Helene.

HELENE. Take care of yourself, Robert.

ROBERT. You too. Thank you. You. Are… Thanks.

> *(She gives him a huge hug.* **HELENE** *and* **ERIK** *leave.)*

> *(***ROBERT*** stands by the fireplace. He turns it on. He stares. He sits in his chair. Music begins. He is so so alone. Lights begin to fade. He looks at the covered Jacuzzi. A thought. Wait…? He stands, looking at the Jacuzzi.)*

> *(blackout)*

End of Play